D1034463

The Valley of Deer

The Valley of Deer

Eileen Dunlop

Holiday House/New York

© Eileen Dunlop 1989
First published by Oxford University Press in 1989
First American publication 1989 by Holiday House
Printed in the United States of America

Library of Congress Cataloging-in-Publication Data

Dunlop, Eileen.
The valley of deer / Eileen Dunlop.
p.   cm.
Summary: Finding an old family Bible behind a secret door in her
house leads Anne on a quest to solve the mystery surrounding the
death in 1726 of a young Scottish woman accused of witchcraft.
ISBN 0-8234-0766-7
[1. Mystery and detective stories.   2. Witchcraft—Fiction.
3. Scotland—Fiction.]   I. Title.
PZ7.D9214Val   1989
[Fic]—dc 19   89-1931   CIP   AC
ISBN 0-8234-0766-7

For Jean Baird and Edith Lipka,
friends in the Fifties

Contents

The Valley of Deer

1

The Owls' House

For Anne Farrar, it all began on the night when her bedroom wall fell down. Not that this event was so very surprising. The Owls' House, which had the date 1698 carved on the lintel above its door, had stood empty for six years after the farmer who owned it moved to a new bungalow down by the Bay. It had damp in its bones when the Farrars moved in, and, during the recent wet weather, had been soaking up moisture like a sponge. Reaching saturation point on the evening of the twenty-seventh of March, the plaster in Anne's bedroom could stand the strain no longer, and gave way.

They were in the kitchen when it happened, Jenny and Anne eating stew in busy silence, while their parents amiably discussed the mysteries of archaeology which mattered more to them than food. The noise was like a single shot from a rifle over their heads, followed by a low, thunderous rumble as the plaster detached itself, fragmented, and showered on to the floor. Jenny jumped to her feet, and ran out into the dark hallway; her father and mother, looking at each other in weary dismay, got up and followed her. Dr Farrar took with him the kerosene lamp from the table, so that Anne was left eating alone in the firelight. She was not curious enough to leave the warmth of the kitchen, reckoning that she would find out soon enough what had happened. She heard the other three jostling on the narrow, uncarpeted stair, the clatter of Jenny's feet, her mother's voice saying sharply, 'Oh, do mind the lamp, Jenny, please! Do you want to set the house on fire?' Then there was an opening and shutting of doors on the landing above, followed by an excited yelp

1

from Jenny, relishing the drama. 'Look, Mother! It's in Anne's room. The whole wall has fallen down. Gosh, what a mess!'

Anne groaned, and groped her way upstairs to inspect the damage.

The mess was certainly spectacular. Lumps of plaster were strewn everywhere, and the air was opaque with fine dust, which was settling unhurriedly in a white film over the floor-boards, the bed, the desk, the dressing-table and Anne's discarded school uniform, which was draped over a chair beside the bed.

This seemed to annoy Mrs Farrar more than anything else. The house did not belong to her, and was doomed to a worse wetting in four months' time, but she was outraged at the thought of having to pay nearly five pounds for a gym tunic, and six pounds, nineteen shillings and eleven pence for a blazer. Whisking up the red and grey garments from the chair, she went out on to the landing to shake them, while Anne stared in the pale lamplight at the great, uneven area of wooden lath which the fallen plaster had exposed. It seemed to be overgrown by some strange, delicate white vine, beautiful in its way, but sinister, like all living things which never see the light of day.

'What is it?' she asked her father.

'It's called dry rot,' he told her. 'The house is full of it. That's what gives it such a strange smell.'

'Oh, I thought that was Jenny,' Anne could not resist replying, and a fight would have broken out, had not Mrs Farrar reappeared at that moment to announce that, since the room could not possibly be cleaned up until tomorrow, for tonight the two girls would have to sleep together.

'But I don't want to sleep with Jenny,' objected Anne. 'She gets as hot as a pig in the night, and she snores, and pulls the covers off me.'

Stunned by this string of insults, Jenny was momentarily incapable of speech, which allowed her mother to say, 'All right. Sleep on the floor in the scullery if you like. All I'm saying is that you can't sleep here.'

Ungraciously, Anne said she supposed she would share with Jenny, and Jenny said she thought she would rather sleep on the floor in the scullery. Then, because they bickered constantly, but could never remember to sustain a quarrel, they forgot all about it.

Later that night, when she was stepping daintily about her room, trying not to disturb the dust as she collected her nightie and the other bits and pieces she would need, Anne noticed something which intrigued her. Behind the vine, only part of the wall was covered with the wooden laths which had supported the plaster. In the corner, where the damaged wall met the one where the window was, there was the outline of a door. It had been papered over, but it was certainly there. When Anne held up her oil-lamp, she could see clearly the doorposts and the lintel, and a regular depression in the paper where the door was hung, slightly further back. A roughly constructed trellis of wooden strips, taking the place of proper laths, had come away with the plaster, and was now lying broken on the floor.

Anne looked at the door for a moment, then decided not to tell anyone about it. Unless they noticed for themselves, she would keep it a secret, and tomorrow, after the room had been cleaned, she would investigate privately. The spring term at Marymount School had ended that afternoon, three whole weeks of holiday lay ahead, and with Mother showing all the charm of a caged rat, it would only be wise to find occupations which would keep one out of her way.

2

The Jardyne Bible

The night spent in her sister's bed was not as bad as Anne had anticipated. Although she hated Jenny's room, with its clutter of china animals and useless objects decked with ribbon and pink nylon net, once the lamp had been put out she didn't have to look at it. Nor was she tempted to burst out laughing at Jenny, looking incredible in mauve 'baby doll' pyjamas, with her fine red hair rolled into innumerable small sausages, and secured all over her head with metal pins. The smell of Nivea cream was strong, but Anne liked the smell of Nivea.

But, 'Isn't it rather uncomfortable?' she ventured, as Jenny writhed in the darkness, trying to find a tolerable position for her armoured head. Anne had never in her life considered putting curlers in her straight, neatly bobbed fair hair.

'Listen,' said Jenny severely. 'You've got to make an effort. Princess Margaret never got to look the way she does without making an effort, did she?'

'I don't know,' replied Anne truthfully.

'Well, you can take it from me she didn't,' said Jenny, in the tone of one who has inside information. Ever since Queen Elizabeth's Coronation last summer, which she had seen on television, Jenny had been Princess Margaret's most faithful admirer.

As soon as she had succeeded in settling her head comfortably, Jenny fell asleep. Anne, who never slept so easily, lay awake for a while in the darkness which pressed in upon the ancient house and was more absolute than any darkness which city-dwellers know. Born in London in

1940, Anne's earliest experience had been of black-out and blitz, and not until 1946, when the street lamp had begun to shine through her bedroom curtains all night long, had she learned to sleep deeply. Coming to the Owls' House had revived her old fears, but she had soon realized that this was not an expectant, throbbing darkness, liable to be holed with sudden bursts of murderous fire. Now she liked it, finding it pleasant to lie under the blankets, listening to the familiar night sounds, her father's typewriter rattling distantly, the gurgle of primitive plumbing, the creaking of the stair as her mother came up to make sure she and Jenny were in bed, and the oil-lamp safely extinguished.

There was the usual, reassuring, whispered conversation.

'Anne, are you asleep?'

'Not yet.'

'Everything all right?'

'Yes, thank you.'

'Count sheep, then. Good-night, my love.'

She was a good mother, really, for all her funny ways, and if she was behaving like a caged rat, no one could blame her. For the last five weeks, it had never stopped raining. Water had cascaded from a steely sky, filling drains and ditches, flooding the road at the old Witch's Brig, sending the little Water of Deer leaping wildly over its boulders, making whirlpools where normally it slid sedately into Loch Dree. For most people this was a nuisance, rather than a disaster, but Mrs Farrar had come to Scotland for one purpose only, to excavate the Neolithic burial cairn known as the Grey Mound of Deer, and to find herself cooped up indoors, with so much work still to be done on the site, was almost more than she could bear.

For time was beginning to run out. On the fifteenth of August, come what might, the apertures in the great concrete dam which was being built across the eastern end of the Valley would be closed, and the level of the Water of Deer would begin to rise. Then the tiny Loch Dree would push back its banks, and presently the Church, the Manse, the School, the Owls' House, and nineteen cottages would vanish for ever beneath a new loch, part of a great Hydro-Electricity Scheme. For this was 1954, the Second World War was history, and the march of progress had begun. So Mrs Farrar, who was more in love with the past than with the future, was tetchier than usual, and unable to take much interest in unimportant events, like the wrecking of Anne's bedroom.

Shortly after her mother's departure downstairs, Anne heard the athletic footsteps of Ben Martin, the research assistant, running across the wet yard to the cottage where he lived. Then there was silence, broken only by Jenny's catarrhal breathing, the soft whishing of the rain, and the occasional hoot of an owl up in the wood behind the house. Anne lay cosily curled up, thinking about the hidden door, and wondering what lay behind it. How marvellous it would be, she thought, if she opened it, and stepped through the space into a wood, like Lucy in *The Lion, the Witch and the Wardrobe*, which Anne had read when she was younger—although at fourteen and three weeks, she would have preferred to find herself in the enchanted wood of the legends of King Arthur, which were her favourite reading now. But it was much more likely, she knew, that there would only be spiders, and a bad smell.

The sound of the rain had a soothing effect, and presently Anne too fell asleep.

In the morning, after breakfast, the cleaning of Anne's room was organized by Jenny, the only organizing force in a pretty disorganized household. It was thanks to her—and she knew it—that Anne had her stockings darned, that her father had a clean shirt on the days when he had to go to the Museum in Edinburgh, that the family had nourishing meals to supplement the three of Heinz' 57 Varieties—Scotch broth, spaghetti and baked beans—which her mother served up most of the time. Jenny didn't know how her parents would cope when she left home at

Christmas to become a probationer nurse at University College Hospital in London, but she did know that they would be a lot less comfortable. Now, she got out aprons for herself and Anne, and began to issue orders in the pleasantly bossy fashion which had led to her being made Senior Prefect at Marymount after only one term in the school.

'Come on, wake up, Anne! Fill the washing-up bowl with hot water, and get out the scrubbing-brush from under the sink. You'd better bring the packet of Tide, and some Ajax and green soap. I'll fetch the brush and dustpan. And cheer up! A little hard work isn't going to kill you.'

'You'll make a wonderful matron, Jen,' commented Anne sourly. She had just seen her parents disappear briskly into their warm study with the morning paper, and wished she could disappear too. But her irony misfired, as it usually did with Jenny.

'Well, thank you, Anne,' she said, with a gratified smile. She hoped that her efficiency would bring her quick promotion in her chosen profession.

After a couple of hours of hard work, however, sweeping, scouring and shaking bedclothes, the room was back to normal, apart from the hole in the wall. With this, Anne would have to put up, for there was no point in having anything at the Owls' House mended now. Predictably, Jenny did not notice the outline of the door. When she had gone downstairs to start preparing lunch, Anne lay exhausted on her bed for a while, looking at it, and wondering whether she had either the energy or the nerve to open it. She was not afraid of spiders, but on the other hand ... Eventually, banishing rats, corpses and coffins from her mind, she got up and found a paper-knife in the drawer of her desk. Then she set to work to strip away the white growth which covered the door, like the enchanted ivy of a fairy tale.

The vine was clinging to the paper covering by means of tiny suckers. As Anne worked, bits of the thin paper came adrift, revealing patches of cracked brown paint under-neath. Finally, she was able to run her knife around the frame of the door, and the remaining paper fell away, revealing a door made of wooden planks, only a little taller than Anne herself. She knew that it led into a closet, which was called a press in Scotland, and that it could not be deep, because it was set into the thick outer wall of the house. Why it had been papered over, neither she nor anyone else would ever know. The latch had been removed for the sake of smoothness, but there were two holes where it had been, one of them large enough to accommodate Anne's forefinger. With a slight shiver, but no thought now of magic forests, she pulled the door towards her.

There were certainly plenty of spiders. Festoons of grey cobweb hung from the ceiling, and the walls of the shallow closet were also veined with the pale trellis of dry rot. The smell was awful, a rank mix of mouse-droppings, dust, and the unwholesome scent which the dry rot emitted. Anne was repelled, and she had to force herself to go forward, and peer into what had once been a hanging-space for clothes. A few rusty hooks had been screwed into the underside of a narrow, empty shelf, level with Anne's chin; for a moment she thought, with a twinge of disappointment, that there was nothing in the closet at all.

Then, peering down, she saw on the floor a box, a kind of small trunk, made of hard wood, with a hinged lid. It was covered with grime and cobwebs and grains of plaster, and Anne felt reluctant to touch anything so filthy. But curiosity overcame distaste. Bending down, she pulled it out quickly into the light, and shut the closet door. Then she knelt beside it, and used her handkerchief to wipe away the worst of the dirt from the lid.

Opening the box was difficult. The lid—fortunately for the preservation of the contents—fitted very tightly, and Anne had to go downstairs and fetch a screwdriver from the drawer in the scullery. With its help she did manage to pry the lid up, and lifted out a hard, knobbly object, wrapped in a piece of sacking. This was a blackened pewter candlestick, which she laid on her bed. Under it, there was a piece of paper, frail and yellow with age, folded around a tiny curl of flaxen hair. The paper bore the sad explanation, in browned ink, *Haire of my sonne Johnne, dyed 2 yrs and 6 months. 29 Merch 1701.*

The only other object in the box was so large and heavy that Anne had difficulty in lifting it out. When she did, she saw that it was a book, its leather binding blotched with mould. It was falling apart, and the pages, clinging damply together, were so defaced by brown spots that the print was almost impossible to read. But there was no mystery about what the book was. On the spine, in lettering not totally robbed of its gilt, Anne could make out the words, *Holy Bible*, and when she turned back the front cover, she was interested to see that on the flyleaf there was writing. The ink had run, and the clumsy, blotched script was hard to read. But, peering closely through her horn-rimmed spectacles, Anne was able to decipher these words.

Euphan Jardyne   born the 3 Maie 1677   of *Hoolets Fairm*   married *Jennet Schawe* of *Uplawmuir*   the 3 Averill 1697

to thaim born

Euphan Johnne   the 26 Septembre 1698   deid Pasche Day the 29 Merch 1701

Jennet Marie   the 24 Decembre 1699   marryed *Isaac Burness* of *the Lea*   the 3 Februar 1719

Robert   the 15 Januare 1701   marryed *Christian Grahame* of *Dumfriess* toun   the 12 Maie 1722

Alice   the 15 Januare 1701

All of this was in the same heavy, laboured script, as if it had been written by a hand ill used to the task. But then someone else had drawn a pen stroke through the name *Alice*, and written alongside it in a lighter, perhaps more feminine hand, the words, *deid the 24 juin 1726 blottit owt of the Boke of Lyffe.*

Blottit owt of the Boke of Lyffe. Anne stared at these extraordinary words for a long time, unable to understand them, but with an uneasy, growing awareness that they meant something very terrible indeed. To die when you were how old? Only twenty-five, that was bad enough. But to have such harsh, final words written alongside your name, that was something worse still. What had Alice Jardyne done to deserve such an appalling epitaph? Anne sat on her bed for a while, half-hearing through the open window the fretful bleating of sheep in the meadow across the lane, and the gabble of the swollen Water of Deer, hurrying to Loch Dree. But from the past, there was no sound. The Bible of the Jardynes made its statement, and kept its secret.

She was roused by the sound of Jenny's voice on the stair.

'Anne! Come on down—lunch is ready!'

Suddenly feeling very cold, Anne got up and shut the window. But then, imagining Jenny's face if she should come in and see the new mess she had made, she went out quickly and closed the door. She would come back after lunch and clean up, and meanwhile, she would decide whether it was worth while showing her finds to anyone. She knew from experience that her father and mother could not rouse enthusiasm for anything post-dating the Celts, but, at the same time, she felt that she probably ought to tell someone. Things as old as the Bible and candlestick might be valuable, or at least belong to someone who might like to have them back.

3

An Expert Opinion

After lunch, the rain having eased off temporarily, Mrs Farrar and Jenny put on boots and raincoats and set out to walk up Sheardale to Uplawmoor, a farm now high in the hills, but which in a year's time would stand on the new loch's brim. Anne watched them rather regretfully from the kitchen window as they tramped along the lane under a raggy, restless sky. She liked walking in the country, with its unexpected sounds and sights and smells, but she had thought she should make an excuse today. She still had to clear up the floor in her bedroom, and she had decided at lunch-time to show her discoveries to her father. He would not be going walking, since he always spent Saturday afternoon writing his book review for *Archaeology Now*. So she had told her mother that her period was due, and she had a sore tummy, which was on the verge of being true, and when the others were safely out of the way she went upstairs again with the broom and dustpan, and a damp cloth. When she had got rid of the debris, she carried the box and its contents downstairs, and put her head round the study door.

'Daddy, may I interrupt you for a moment?'

'Of course, Anne. I'll be glad of an excuse not to get started.'

'Great. I want to show you something.'

Dr Farrar helped her to bring in her finds from the hall, and cleared a space for them amid mounds of books and papers on the table. He listened with polite interest to the story of how she had found them, and ran his fingers over wood, metal and leather with an archaeologist's tactile appreciation. He looked at the flyleaf on the Bible, and

11

shook his head over the pathetic little lock of hair. But Anne knew that these things did not cause him any inner excitement. To him, a Bible of 1700 was merely modern, and he would have preferred a prehistoric collar-bone any day. Not that this offended her. She did not want his congratulations, only answers to two questions, which she now put to him. To whom did these objects now belong, and—to her, much more important—what could a person possibly have done to deserve to be blotted out of the Book of Life? Whatever it meant, the bleak despair of that phrase was making a cold place in Anne's mind, and the name 'Alice Jardyne' along with it.

When he had finished running his hands over the box, which he obviously liked best, Dr Farrar sat down in one of the shabby armchairs by the fire, and waved Anne towards the other. She and Jenny were not usually invited to come into the study, and when they were, were treated more like guests than daughters. Dr Farrar looked at Anne with shrewd, pleasant eyes, which were surrounded by a net of wrinkles, as if he were constantly screwing them up to peer at things which were very fascinating, and very small.

'There's no problem answering your first question,' he told her. 'They belong to the owner of this house, our landlord. Not that he'll be much interested in them, I dare say. Ex-army type, man of today, no interest in the past at all. Delighted for us to pay rent for his ruin, but thinks your Ma and Pa are nuts.'

'Did he actually say so?' asked Anne, amused. 'Most people are too polite.' Then, 'I thought he was a farmer.'

Dr Farrar grinned.

'Of a sort,' he conceded.

'What sort?'

'The sort who milks his cows with kid gloves on.'

'Is he rich?'

'I'll say.'

'I see,' said Anne. 'Will you tell him he's richer by a Bible, a candlestick and a wisp of hair?'

'When I see him.'

12

'And the answer to my other question?'

Dr Farrar threw another log on to the fire, stretched out his long legs across the hearthrug, and made a cautious gesture with his brown hands.

'That's not so easy,' he admitted. 'The words come from Revelation, the last book of the Bible. The writer tended to go in for language which nowadays we'd find a bit exaggerated. Sinners were to be blotted out of the Book of Life—and cast into the Lake of Fire, if I remember correctly. As for what the poor girl had done—like many questions of history, the truth is probably buried with her. But I'd say the most likely explanation is that she got herself pregnant by some chap who wouldn't marry her, and died in childbirth. The Scots of that period were puritanical beyond belief, and such a thing was a dreadful disgrace in a family.'

'Bad enough to deserve having such a hateful thing said about you?' asked Anne incredulously.

'Lord, yes,' replied her father. 'That kind of language didn't seem exaggerated to them. They really believed in hell-fire, you see, and you didn't have to do much to deserve it. A nasty, dour, uncharitable lot they were. Now—is there anything else, or may I get on with my review, please, ma'am?'

Which was the end of the interview, but Anne was far from satisfied. She took the box and its contents back up to her room, and spent most of the next hour poring over the words on the flyleaf of the Bible, memorizing the names and dates, working out ages, wondering about the faceless folk whom the names represented. She noticed that the date of Euphan Johnne's death, Easter Day 1701, tallied with that on the paper wrapped around the lock of hair, and supposed that the writing must have been that of his mother, Jennet Schawe, who had become Mrs Jardyne. And she presumed that the recording of the names had been done by his father, Euphan Jardyne—a man not much used to writing, judging by his awkward lettering.

Neither of these, at least, had written of their daughter, *blottit owt of the Boke of Lyffe*—although, Anne thought, they would be the people most disgraced if Alice had indeed had an illegitimate child. These hateful words had been written by a third person, and there was no clue at all to that person's identity. Even Anne's suspicion that the writing was a woman's might, she knew, be a false one.

When she heard her mother and Jenny coming back through the yard, she packed away the Bible, the hair and the candlestick in the box, and pushed it under her bed. There it must remain until Dr Farrar contacted his landlord, and found out what he wanted done with it. Then Anne went downstairs, feeling sadly that she had very quickly come to a dead end. And, quite soon, another, spectacular discovery was to make hers seem very small fry indeed.

4

Miss Bones

As if the deluge of the last month had not been enough, April that year began with a blizzard, a sudden white-out of the Valley, the last it would experience until the end of time. Next winter, the bare hills would raise frosty heads above a wide, black expanse of water, instead of a snow-bound valley bottom. For the last time, the road was blocked at either end of the village, and masses of snow overhung walls and roofs, like bedclothes falling off the bed. But then, after three days, the wind blew from the west, the sky shone clear and bright, and the snow slipped away. A few days after that, the ground around the Grey Mound was dry enough to allow the elder Farrars to resume their excavations, and Mrs Farrar's temper improved accordingly.

On Friday morning, at the end of the first holiday week, Jenny and Anne went on the bus to Dumfries, to spend the day. They did some shopping, had a snack lunch at a coffee bar, and went to the cinema in the afternoon. Coming rather wearily up the farm road on the way home, they looked for their parents in the field opposite the house; now that the weather had got so much better, Dr and Mrs Farrar were usually out there from early morning until nightfall, tweed-clad and wind-blown, crawling and prowling with their trowels and tape-measures around the gaunt pile of grey boulders which was the remains of a chambered tomb four thousand years old. More often than not, Ben Martin was there too, in his fawn duffle-coat and striped university scarf, under orders to move stones, carry buckets of earth, and be ready with the tape-measure. But today, remarkably, the tomb seemed to be deserted.

15

'Don't tell me *they've* gone to the flicks,' said Jenny, making an astonished face, as they turned in at the back gate of the Owls' House.

Anne grinned appreciatively at this.

'If they have, it will be to see *The Curse of the Mummy's Tomb*,' she replied. 'But look—here's Ben. He'll be able to tell us.' As she spoke, Ben Martin, in an old red sweater and corduroy trousers, slithered through the kitchen doorway. He had a dazed expression on his face. 'Listen, Ben,' continued Anne. 'Our parents seem to have disappeared.'

The reply was memorable.

'They're upstairs in Jenny's bedroom. They've found a skeleton, and they're putting it together on the bed.'

With a howl of anguish, Jenny fled indoors.

Unable to help giggling, Anne left Ben and followed, through the kitchen and up the dark stair. As she emerged on to the landing, she could hear Jenny's voice, wailing complaint.

'But it isn't fair. Why does it have to be my room? Why can't it go in Anne's? I'm not going to sleep with a skeleton.'

And then there was her mother's, cool and unconcerned.

'Don't be silly, Jenny. No one's asking you to sleep with it. It's just that this is the only room in the house with decent light, and what we're doing is very important. You can sleep with Anne for a bit, can't you?'

This quickly wiped the smile off Anne's face, as in an instant she visualized her tidy room littered with china dogs and crinolined dolls and jars of Pond's cold cream.

'Hell's teeth,' she muttered, and kicked the bath savagely as she stowed the things they had bought in Dumfries in the bathroom cabinet. 'Hell's teeth, and buckets of blood.'

Then she shut her mouth in a tight line, and went glumly into Jenny's room to view the bones.

To most people, the scene in the small, coomed bedroom would have been a bizarre one, but to Jenny and Anne, who had lived all their lives with experts on Neolithic

16

remains, bones were as unremarkable as pieces of flint. Jenny was neither revolted nor frightened by skeletons; it was the inconvenience she objected to, and the suspicion that ancient bones must be unhygienic. Anne generally found bones interesting, although she agreed with Jenny that one should wash one's hands after handling them, and before cooking the supper.

Dr Farrar and his wife had put a large wooden board on the bed, and covered it with a sheet of green oilcloth. Referring constantly to photographs taken that morning of the skeleton lying in the innermost chamber of the tomb, and developed by Ben in the larder, they were lifting frail, porous bones very delicately from a long wooden box, and reconstructing the figure on the board. Already the skull was there, the collar-bone, the shoulder-bones, part of the spine, the breast-bone, the bones of the upper right arm. There were chalk marks sketched lightly on the oilcloth, indicating the parts which were, at present, missing.

Anne had come in determined to show her annoyance by feigning boredom, but, inconveniently, the sight of the two dishevelled figures, bent raptly over their absurd task, brought on one of the rushes of love which she sometimes felt for them, and she could not bring herself to spoil their fun.

Instead, 'Is it going well?' she asked her mother, who was standing on one leg, like a stork. Even an eminent archaeologist could have a painful bunion.

Mrs Farrar, whose long, brown-eyed face had exactly the same expression of shrewd concentration as her husband's, straightened her back, carefully put down her foot, and smiled at Anne.

'Very,' she said.

'Is it really important, Mother?'

Mrs Farrar pushed back wisps of brown-and-grey hair from her high forehead, looked at the bones on the board, and said, 'Yes. I really think it is. It's certainly the best-preserved skeleton that's come to light in excavations in this part of the world, so far. Cremated bones are much more common.'

'Is it a Mr or a Miss?' Anne wanted to know.

'Miss. Or Mrs,' replied her mother.

'How do you know?'

'By the skull, and the pelvis. The measurements are different,' explained Mrs Farrar. 'Ageing is a different matter, of course. She might have been anything between eighteen and thirty-five.'

'Why thirty-five?' asked Anne, really interested now. 'Why not sixty?'

'Oh, she'd never have lived to be sixty. Thirty-five was old for people who lived the way she did,' her mother explained. 'However—you'll also be interested in something we found with her, I think. Daddy will tell you at supper, if we're having any. Go and talk nicely to Jenny, Anne. Tell her I'm old and tired, and ask her to heat up the frying-pan.'

'That's asking a lot, in the circumstances,' Anne told her severely. 'But I'll see what I can do.'

It was as she was going downstairs in the dark that Anne had a sudden, chilly remembrance of Alice Jardyne. She had not previously thought of her that day. It was not only in Neolithic times, she remembered, that people had died young. Alice Jardyne had only been twenty-five.

5

A Small Red Herring

Jenny expressed outrage, and banged about a bit, but she cooked the supper, as both her mother and Anne had known she would. At seven o'clock, with a huffy but virtuous expression on her freckled face, she called her parents from their skeleton, and Anne from her room, where she had been resignedly clearing a space for Jenny's clothes in the wardrobe. They found their way by their noses to the supper of sausages, eggs and fried tomatoes, toast, plum jam and Fuller's walnut cake, which Jenny had spread on a blue cloth on the kitchen table. With the wood fire jumping up the chimney, and the darkening Valley shut out behind striped curtains which Jenny had made, the room appeared cosy and cheerful, the kerosene lamp on the table for once more picturesque than inconvenient.

Suddenly aware of hunger, everyone fell silently to eating. Only Anne, glancing round the familiar family faces, remembered with a cold inner pang that in a matter of months this house would lie fathoms deep in icy water, still a real house, but drowned, in impenetrable darkness, with its memories of two and a half centuries of human life. Fish would swim mindlessly among the twisted branches of sun-starved apple trees in the orchard, while weed drifted eerily over the silent grey burial-place in the meadow, across the lane. Anne knew that as a Londoner, who had always taken such things for granted, she had no right to object to the desire of country people for electric light, vacuum cleaners and television sets. But she did wish they could have acquired them some other way. To her, the death of a valley was a horrible prospect, and sometimes, when she woke in the night, the thought of it swept over her like a sad, cold sigh.

To shut it out now, she said, 'Daddy, what did you find in the tomb, besides the skeleton? Mother said you'd tell us at supper.'

'Quite right,' agreed her father. He put down his knife and fork, and slipped his hand into the pocket of his tweed jacket. 'Here, take a squint at this,' he continued, and passed across the table to Anne a round object, which fitted coolly into the palm of her right hand.

'What on earth?' said Anne, in surprise, as she held it to the lamp, and peered at it in the thin gold light.

The thing she held was a smooth ball of clear crystal, about the size of a small tomato, contained within four curving strips of tarnished metal, which she supposed was silver. Where the strips converged on top of the ball, there was a metal loop, through which one might have passed a chain, or a leather thong. Anne could see lettering engraved on the metal, but she could not begin to decipher it in the lamp's weak light. She put the object into Jenny's impatient hand, and turned with raised eyebrows to her father.

'How very odd,' she said. 'Of course it isn't Neolithic—but what is it? And how could it possibly have come to be in the tomb, beside the skeleton?'

'Actually, it wasn't beside the skeleton,' Dr Farrar told her, as he spread plum jam on a slice of toast. 'You know how the tomb is constructed, with an entrance passage, and beyond it two chambers, one leading into the other?' Anne nodded. 'Well, this thing was lying on the floor in the first chamber, just outside the door of the second, where we found our Miss Bones. We were just getting ready to move the last of the stones from the doorway of the inner chamber—an exciting enough moment, in all conscience —when your mother kicked it, and it rolled.'

'That's right. I thought it was just another stone at first,' put in Mrs Farrar, who was cutting slices of walnut cake which she considered large enough to be generous, and small enough to be prudent, in these cautious post-rationing days. 'But there was something about the way it rolled that alerted me, and I picked it up. I was very surprised.'

'But how did it get there?' demanded Jenny. She was not in the least interested in archaeology, and usually expressed her disapproval of her parents' shop-talk by ignoring it. But this was so mysterious that, for the moment, she had even forgotten that she was supposed to be in a huff with them. 'Even I know it isn't Stone Age,' she went on. 'It would be quite pretty, really, if it was polished up—not like your usual flint choppers and bits of flowerpot.'

'What do you think, Anne?' asked Mrs Farrar, appealing to the more sympathetic of her daughters.

'I suppose,' said Anne, who had got hold of the glassy ball again, and was fingering it thoughtfully, 'it means that someone, some time, got into the tomb and dropped it. Were there any signs of a break-in?'

Mrs Farrar shook her head.

'None,' she said. 'Certainly, no one could have got in the way we did, down the passage and through the first chamber into the second. It's taken months to clear the outer covering of the cairn, as you know, and take out all the stones they'd used to block the way in. We'd both swear they'd never been disturbed before. However, it does seem possible that someone very thin and small could have got in through the roof of the outer chamber. There was a space between two of the roof slabs that a child, or a very undersized adult, even, might have wriggled through.'

'And got out again?' asked Jenny.

'They'd have had to,' answered her father. 'There was no other way out. It would have been more difficult, though.'

A horrible thought entered Anne's mind.

'Daddy,' she whispered, her blue eyes widening. 'You don't suppose—the skeleton——'

'No,' said Dr Farrar very firmly, because he knew his Anne. 'That is absolutely impossible. The ball wasn't in the same section as the skeleton, and anyway, you can trust

Ma and Pa to know prehistoric bones when they see them. Whoever got in, got out. It's just possible, of course, that the ball was dropped into the tomb through the roof-space, accidentally or on purpose. Less likely, I suppose, but possible.'

'What I hate about history,' complained Jenny, 'is all these "likelys" and "possiblys" and "supposes". You spend your whole lives asking questions that don't have any proper answers.'

No one paid any attention to this. They had heard it all, many, many times. Anne, reassured that no one had been trapped and died in the tomb, sat for a while in silence, liking the cold, mysterious feel of the ball in her hand. Presently she asked, 'Does either of you have any idea what it is?'

'Yes, I do,' said her mother. 'I saw an almost identical one once in a castle up north, in Inverness-shire. It was supposed to be a talisman—a charm-stone, you know, that had the power to cure sickness in cattle, and probably in humans too. And there was some nonsense about its owner being able to see into the future—the usual superstitious claptrap of an unscientific age. The tradition was that it had been brought back to Scotland by Crusaders, but that wasn't likely, either. That kind of silversmithing is seventeenth century—about the same period as that junk you found in the cupboard, Anne. The balls are fairly ordinary geological specimens.'

All very dismissive, as Anne recognized, but she persisted, 'So—it couldn't have been dropped in the tomb before—say 1600?'

'1650, I'd have thought,' replied Mrs Farrar.

'I see.' Anne sensed that her mother's attitude to the crystal ball was exactly the same as her father's had been to the Bible and the candlestick. To them, the seventeenth century was yesterday. 'What are you going to do with it?' she wanted to know.

'Oh, it will have to go to the Museum in Edinburgh, along with all our other finds. It's only a curiosity, of course, and a small red herring, as far as our work is concerned.'

Anne could see that Mrs Farrar was fast losing interest in the topic of the crystal ball. She was desperate to get back to her bones. Anne was interested in her parents' work, and had recently made up her mind that she too would be an archaeologist when she grew up. But it did occur to her occasionally that they were a rather narrow-minded couple.

'May I keep it for a while?' she asked.

'Oh, certainly, if you want to,' agreed Mrs Farrar, as she drained her coffee cup and pushed back her chair from the table. 'But don't lose it, and remember, there's to be no growling when we want to have it back.'

That night, influenced, she afterwards supposed, by the finding of the skeleton, Anne had a dream so vivid that it seemed to have the authority of a waking experience.

It began with her standing on the edge of a place she knew well. It was a little area of virgin oakwood, on a hillside above the Owls' House, a glade carpeted with moss and the decayed leaves of many autumns. It was like a grey and russet island on a dark sea of spruce. Only—strangely—there now seemed to be no spruce, just an extension all round of the rather feeble oaks, with frilly patches of grey sky caught in their leaves. It was not as dark as Anne thought it ought to be, but she was aware of cold, and knew that it was just after sunrise.

She also knew that fear was in the air. There was no sound in the wood near to hand, no chirp of waking bird, no scutter of tiny beast, no breath of wind, even. But beyond the uncanny stillness, Anne could hear a commotion. Some hunt was up, and coming closer. As she strained her ears, she heard a distant crashing in the undergrowth, uncontrolled whoops of male laughter, a pale flicker of torches no longer needed to give light. The clamour drew nearer, and suddenly Anne saw the quarry break out of a gorse thicket somewhere to the right, and run towards her. But this was no fox, or hunted hare; it was a young woman in a torn and muddied brown garment, the skimpy skirt of which she was holding up in her right hand. Anne could see bare, bleeding brown legs, and feet so terribly lacerated that it made her feel sick to look at them.

She raised her eyes pityingly, and found herself staring into a small, tanned face with a large nose and dark eyes hard with pain and despair. The broad forehead was dirty with mud and blood, and the black hair streaming around the thin cheeks was as ragged as the dress. Anne had no idea who this was, or why she was being pursued, but in a moment of intense compassion she wanted to help her, more than she had ever wanted anything in her life. Yet she knew that it was impossible.

Blind with terror, the girl came stumbling towards her, seeming to pass so closely that Anne could see the glistening sweat on her brow, and hear the harsh sobbing of her breath. Then suddenly she wheeled away to the left, and struck out again, down through the wood to where the Owls' House was.

Anne never saw the hunters. Overcome with horror, she turned her face away, and when she looked again, she was in a room full of darkness.

6

In Hoolets' Wood

Next morning Anne took the charm-stone into the low-roofed scullery at the back of the house. There she found a tin of metal polish and a piece of rag, and began patiently to rub away the tarnish which coated the strips of metal. It took a long time, and in the end she was unable to get the loop on top perfectly clean. But she decided that it would have to do. When she had cleared up, she took the stone to the window, and, holding it to the light, read the words which were engraved along the silver bands. *In nomine patris et filii et spiritus sancti.* Anne had more than enough Latin to know that this meant, *In the name of the Father, and of the Son, and of the Holy Spirit.* She thought the words conventional and disappointing; she had been hoping for something which might hint at the stone's origin, and perhaps even reveal its owner's name.

But then, because Jenny was spring-cleaning the kitchen, and would be sure to want her to help, Anne put on her overcoat, and slipped surreptitiously out of the back door. She would go for a walk, since she wanted peace to think; no one could think while balancing on a step-ladder, washing high shelves, with Jenny zealously shouting instructions from the floor.

After the snow, the warm wind had continued to blow, and the late spring of the north had come like the crack of a whip. Only on the high uplands were there still white streaks, daily diminishing. Further down, there were pale green knobs on the spruce trees, the spearheads of the daffodils had tilted and turned lemon, and there was the tenderest speckle of leaf on the hedges along the lane. Not that Anne was in a noticing mood; as she trudged up through the fields to the wood above the house, her mind was occupied with her dream of the night before. Anne was intelligent enough to know that dreams are often connected with waking experiences, and—coming immediately after the exciting discovery of the skeleton—it did not occur to her to doubt a link between the two. Normally she would have dismissed the dream as the consequence of the excitement. But it had not been like the dreams she usually had, without substance or sequence, and often so absurd that she knew she was dreaming even before she woke up. Last night's dream, on the contrary, had been so vivid, the action so compelling, that Anne felt she had witnessed something which had actually happened. Common sense told her that this was ridiculous, but had not stopped her putting some questions to her father at breakfast-time. As usual, she had received no very positive replies.

'Daddy, have you any idea what Miss Bones looked like? And what sort of clothes she would have worn?'

'Not really, Anne. She was just under five feet in height, had prominent cheekbones and a receding forehead. Her left arm is missing, but that doesn't necessarily mean she didn't have one. There are other parts missing too, and until we get more work done on the floor of the chamber, we won't know how much has just disintegrated. And there's no way of telling how prehistoric people dressed. All the pictures you see are conjectural.'

'Fur?' suggested Anne.

'Presumably.'

'Cloth?'

'We really know nothing about their dressmaking skills. No fabric could possibly have survived so long in this climate, you see. Why do you want to know this, Anne?'

'I had a dream about her,' Anne replied.

Dr Farrar said something about dreams not providing very reliable information about the appearance of unknown individuals. Anne was tempted to retort that the same was apparently true of archaeology, but decided not to. She liked a peaceful life, and knew that the pleasure of

26

parent-baiting was never worth the crossness it generated. As she helped Jenny wash up, she had a moment of elation, remembering that the girl in the dream had been holding up her skirt only with her right hand. If this was because she did not have a left arm, might it not be evidence that she was Miss Bones? But then, the sheer implausibility of the connection she was making deflated her again. Was she really suggesting, she asked herself sternly, that she had dreamed of something which had *actually happened* in this remote Scottish valley, four thousand years ago, to a nameless girl whose pathetic remains now lay on a board in Jenny's bedroom? Firmly, she ordered herself to put such nonsense out of her mind.

But that was more easily said than done, and as she climbed a stile, and jumped over a spring that was gushing silver between limp tussocks of last year's grass, Anne admitted to herself that it was what she was suggesting—indeed believed. From where else could such a vision possibly have come? She could think of no incident she had ever witnessed in real life or on film, no story she had read, no conversation between her parents about Stone Age people, which could have caused her to dream of that terrible chase.

Seeing again in memory's eye the ominous, flickering torches, and the exhausted girl with her terrified, animal eyes, Anne walked slowly down the springy brown path through the spruce trees, and, without thinking where she was going, emerged from the evergreen into the little clump of oak called Hoolets' Wood. 'Hoolets' was an old Scots word for owls. Anne knew that this was a tiny fragment of the great oak forest which had clothed this countryside from prehistoric times until the seventeenth century. Now the trees were little and spindly with age, and even in summer their leaves were as sparse as old men's hair. This was where it had happened, of course. The same wood, a different season of the year. Down this ride, the girl had come running . . . Suddenly feeling tired out, Anne sat down on a fallen tree trunk to rest, unthinkingly took the crystal charm-stone out of her pocket, and had her second astonishing experience in the space of twelve hours.

For as she sat there, it came to her that she had made a mistake. Her preoccupation with the skeleton had led her thoughts in a wrong direction. Now, she felt assured, the brown girl of the dream had not been a prehistoric figure at all. She had been Alice Jardyne, and the terrible thing that was happening in the dream had once, long ago, happened to her. It did not matter that Anne had even less evidence of Alice Jardyne's appearance than she had of the skeleton-girl's. She was sure that this was the truth of the matter. And, on grounds equally impossible to prove, she was convinced of something else. The inspiration of her dream had not been the discovery of ancient bones at all, but the discovery of the charm-stone, which had spent the night under her pillow, and which was now tightly clutched in the palm of her right hand.

If you think you have seen a ghost, no amount of assurance by others that you have not is likely to change your mind. It is the same with any strange or irrational experience. People may laugh, or tap their foreheads, or try to reason with you; you know what happened and they do not, so that, for you, is the end of the matter. This was how Anne felt now, as she plunged down through the sodden undergrowth to the path through the fields. The idea that she had in her possession a stone of power was a stunning one, of course, but she accepted it unquestioningly, and no one that day could possibly have talked her out of her conviction.

Not—as she told herself firmly—that anyone would have the opportunity to try. Anne knew the people she lived with far too well to risk sharing with any of them a whisper of what had happened to her in the wood. No matter how sure she was that the charm-stone, believed long ago to foretell the future, had on this occasion told her something from the past, no one she knew would ever agree with her. She remembered what her mother had called such beliefs, 'the usual superstitious claptrap of an unscientific age'. This was 1954, in a very scientific age, and her parents were very scientific people, who never had time to read a novel, and believed in nothing they could not see and touch. Indeed, Mrs Farrar disapproved of Anne's absorption in the *Tale of King Arthur* as much as she would have disapproved of her reading *Film Fun* and the *Dandy*. King Arthur would be blamed for what had happened to Anne in the wood, and her parents would mutter about her credulity, and how they thought they had brought her up to have more sense. While Jenny, who had inherited her parents' scepticism without their brains, would smile condescendingly, and look superior. It would be intolerable.

But all the same, Anne thought, as she joined the main road, and tramped back towards the village under a bright, windy spring sky, she could not possibly allow the matter to rest there. A week ago, she had never heard the name 'Alice Jardyne', yet in that week it had become as familiar to her as the names of her own friends. She had thought about Alice Jardyne, speculated about her, feared for her, and now, through the power of an ancient stone, was convinced that she had witnessed a terrible incident from her otherwise hidden life. However costly, however painful the knowledge might be, Anne wanted to know more about this girl—who she was, how she had lived, what train of events had brought her, one chill summer morning, to the condition of a hunted beast. Here in the Valley of Deer it had happened; here, if anywhere, the clues to the mystery must lie.

The trouble was that Anne had no idea where to start. Perhaps the stone which had revealed a little might reveal more, but there was no knowing if, or when, it would. Anne did not feel that she could wait on the off chance of another revelation; her instinct told her that she would also have to try more conventional means of finding out. But how? The Bible had stated the year of Alice's beginning, and the year of her end, and had made one harsh, cruel comment on her destiny. Of her twenty-five years of life, it told nothing at all. Anne walked along the ochre verge with her hands in her pockets, frowning into the wind and trying to think of a way forward. For a very long time, not a single idea came to mind.

Only when she came level with the Owls' House, and saw Ben Martin in the field opposite, busy with pegs and tape-measure around the Grey Mound, did a possibility occur to her. Ben might be able to help. Of course, she could not tell him about her experience in Hoolets' Wood, any more than she could tell her own family, but, if she were careful with her questions, he might tell her where to find out some of the things she wanted to know. The thesis which was to make Ben 'Dr Martin' was about Neolithic tombs, but he was—unlike the elder Farrars—a mine of information on subjects ranging from pigs and wild flowers to cricket and railway engines. Jenny was in love with him in a mild, flirty kind of way; Anne did not suppose that Ben, or anyone else, could be in love with Jenny. Anyway, Anne decided, as she waved to him and turned in at the gate, she would go over to his cottage after lunch, and consult him. It would be nice to talk to someone who wasn't itching visibly to turn his attention to a jigsaw of human bones.

7

Church Matters

Before she went downstairs for lunch, Anne found, in an old chocolate-box where she kept her odds and ends, a silver-plated chain with a small enamel pendant on it. It had been a cousin's birthday present, but she had rarely worn it. She slipped the tawdry pendant off the chain, and threaded on the beautiful, mysterious charm-stone in its place. If she were to be the guardian of something so ancient and, apparently, powerful, she wanted to keep it where she could feel it, and not have to be constantly putting a panicky hand into her pocket, fearing its loss. She fastened the chain round her neck, and pushed the stone under the collar of her jersey. Then, after she had swept a clutter of face-powder, scent-bottles, curlers and brushes off her desk and on to Jenny's half of the bed, she clattered down to the kitchen. There was spam, baked beans and an apple sponge for lunch, not the worst meal ever served by Mrs Farrar. After she had eaten her share, Anne let the wind blow her across the yard to Ben's cottage, one of several ramshackle buildings huddled in the lee of the old farmhouse.

When they had arrived, in the summer of 1953, Ben had been given the opportunity to live at the Owls' House, as a temporary member of the Farrar family. He had declined tactfully, saying that he preferred to have a place, however humble, of his own. So Dr Farrar had given him one. It was very humble indeed, with cracks in its windows and a rusty corrugated-iron roof, but Ben had made it comfortable, with shelves for his books and a couple of battered leather armchairs, which he had bought at an auction over at Wigtown. Jenny had made him curtains with the material left over from the kitchen, and both she and Anne thought that, despite the smell of former occupants which caused it to be called the Hens' House, Ben's was a much more attractive residence than their own.

When Anne arrived, lugging the Jardyne Bible in its sacking coat, Ben had just finished washing up lunch in the tiny lean-to scullery at the back of the cottage. Since he was not again required to work on the dig until Monday, he was looking forward to a spell of uninterrupted work on his thesis. But he greeted Anne as if he were pleased to see her, made her a cup of Nescafé, and perched on the table, looking at her with his cheeky brown eyes.

'What can I do for you, Sunshine?' he enquired.

Anne unwrapped the Bible and showed it to him, explaining how she had found it. She pointed out the name of Alice Jardyne on the soiled flyleaf, and the words which always made her feel chilly when she thought about them.

'Daddy thinks she had an illegitimate baby, and her family disowned her,' she told him, 'but I don't feel there's any proof of that. I want to investigate, and see if I can find out what really happened. I thought you could help me, Ben.'

Ben, who had been bending over the Bible, straightened up suddenly, a comical expression of alarm crossing his wind-tanned face.

'Have a heart, Annie,' he implored. 'I'm five months behind with my thesis, and you may have noticed I don't have a lot of time for helping other historians. Why don't you ask Tich and Sadie?'

It always made Anne giggle when Ben referred to her parents as 'Tich and Sadie'. Part of her was amused, part slightly shocked by such levity. For although she lived with them, and found them as ridiculous as most fourteen-year-olds find their parents, she was also aware that they were Titus and Sarah Farrar, the well-known archaeologists, who wrote books, and gave talks on the wireless, and had appeared on television in *The Brains Trust*, and the archaeology quiz programme, *Animal, Vegetable, Mineral?* The students who came to the house in London were very polite and deferential. Not, Anne had noticed, that Ben ever called them 'Tich and Sadie' when he thought there was the least danger of their overhearing him. He called Dr Farrar 'Sir', and Mrs Farrar 'Dr Farrar'. It was from Ben that Anne had learned that Sadie, despite her bunions, was a more distinguished archaeologist than Tich.

Now she giggled, as usual, but hastened to reassure him.

'It's all right. I don't want you actually to do anything—just advise me about where I ought to look. I haven't a clue, and there's no point asking Mother or Daddy—they couldn't care less about anything that isn't prehistoric. I thought I'd ask you because you're more broad-minded, Ben.'

'Thanks, Annie. If it wasn't for my broad mind, I'd maybe be able to concentrate on the contents of my bucket,' said Ben ruefully.

But Anne saw him looking relieved, and she felt sorry for him.

'I won't be a nuisance,' she promised. 'Just tell me how to get started.'

'Well, let me see.' Ben slid down from the table into an armchair, running rough fingers through his spiky black hair. 'First, a wee word of caution, Annie.'

'What?'

'I think you should keep in mind that you may never find out anything at all. The vast majority of the human beings who have ever lived have been blotted out of the Book of Life, in the sense that they've disappeared, and left no trace of their real selves behind. Take Tich and Sadie's skeleton, now. Finding it will increase our understanding of Neolithic people in general, but we'll never know anything about the woman herself. She must have been somebody important to be buried in that way—we know that kind of burial was normally reserved for men, and chiefs of the tribes at that. But we'll never even know her name. As for your lady—you do have a name, of course, and in a sense knowing a name always makes someone more real. But it's unlikely she was a person of any importance, and she may

33

well have taken all her secrets with her when she died—just like Madame Skeleton.'

'So you think it's hopeless,' said Anne disconsolately.

'No, not at all,' Ben replied. 'I just don't want you to be too surprised, or disappointed, if you draw a blank. That doesn't mean I don't think you should try, if you're interested. The name Jardine is a fairly common one in these parts—the churchyard at Deer is full of them. And if you want to find out anything from the past in a place like this, you should begin by looking at the Parish Records. If I were you, I'd go and talk to the Minister.'

So, the following afternoon, Anne did.

The tiny, gaunt, grey Kirk of Deer stood at the centre of the village, dwarfed absurdly by the Manse, which stood next to it. By far the largest building in the district, this was a rather fine, three-storeyed Georgian house, set in two acres of neglected garden. On their arrival, Dr and Mrs Farrar had been entertained to dinner by the Minister and his wife, but no friendship had developed. The Farrars did not go to church, worked on the dig on Sundays, and had given offence by saying they were too busy to talk about their work at a meeting of the Church Women's Guild.

None the less, the Rev. Mr Russell received Anne pleasantly in his book-lined study, and listened with unfeigned interest to her story. He agreed that Dr Farrar's theory of the illegitimate child was probably correct, and in answer to Anne's indignant comment that it wasn't very nice to talk about blotting people out of the Book of Life, however much you disapproved of their behaviour, said mildly that in 1726 people used stronger language than they were nowadays inclined to do. He was a small, fair man, with a rosy face above his dog-collar, and calm, untroubled blue eyes. It was his air of knowing all the answers which riled Mrs Farrar, even more than his suggestion that her concern for social justice must, because she was middle-class, be insincere.

'Ben thought you might let me see the Parish Records,'

said Anne, deciding that this was not the time to have an argument. 'I'd like to find out more about Alice Jardyne, and he says it's just possible she might be mentioned there.'

But the answer was disappointing.

'I'm afraid you'd have to go to Edinburgh for that, Anne. All the old records and minutes are kept at the Scottish Record Office—too valuable to leave lying in the vestry cupboard. We only have the books here covering the last thirty years or so. What I can show you is a copy of the Register of Baptisms, Marriages and Burials in the Parish prior to 1855. It goes back to 1600, when written records began. And I have a book of my own which might interest you—although I suppose the chance of your lady's being mentioned is fairly remote.'

He got up from his chair, padded over to a bookcase, and tipped down a fat, cloth-bound volume, which he put into Anne's lap. 'It was published before the war by the Deer and District Antiquarian Society,' he told her, 'and it's a gem. It's a hotch-potch of people and happenings in the Valley, taken from a lot of sources, including the Parish Records. Fascinating stuff, if you're interested in Valley history. Sad to think it will all end in August, after so many centuries.'

'Yes,' agreed Anne, repressing a little shiver which had nothing to do with the chill of the inadequately heated room. She looked at the title on the spine of the book, *A Book of Deer*, and asked, 'May I borrow this?'

'Certainly,' said Mr Russell. 'I don't expect I'll be needing it, now that I've finished writing the script for the Pageant.'

'What Pageant is that?' asked Anne, as she got up.

'The Pageant of Deer, that we're going to stage in June,' Mr Russell explained. 'We got up a Committee in the winter—we asked your mother to be a member, actually, but she said she was too busy. We felt it was a pity not to mark the end of the community in some way, and this was the idea the Committee came up with—that we should have a historical Pageant, telling the story of the Valley through the ages. It's to be performed on Saturday the twenty-third of June, in the afternoon; then in the evening we're going to have a Midsummer Bonfire up on Cairn-shee, like they used to have in the old days.'

'I see. Who's going to act in the Pageant?' asked Anne, her interest quickening. She liked plays, and had been a keen member of the Drama Club at her grammar school in London.

'Oh, anyone who wants to, really,' said the Minister. 'We need all the actors and actresses we can get. My wife's agreed to be the producer, and she'll be casting parts in the Church Hall on Tuesday. Why don't you and your sister come along, Anne? It would be nice to see the Farrars taking part in a village activity.'

Well, honestly, Anne thought irritably. Could the man never leave well alone? But she was grateful to him for his help, and she rather liked the Pageant idea, so she swallowed her annoyance and said, 'Well, we might, if we're allowed. I'll speak to Jen when I get home. Thank you for lending me the book.'

And when she had arranged to meet him in the vestry the next morning, so that he could show her the Register of Baptisms, Marriages and Burials, she said goodbye, buttoned up her tweed overcoat, and went out into the breezy afternoon.

Anne's most convenient way home was through the old graveyard, long disused, which surrounded the little church. Sheltered from the road by a high wall, it was a peaceful place, with daffodils, and worn grey stones listing like sails in a sea of winter grass. Anne, who was the kind of person who could never resist reading anything in print, wandered for a while among the hummocks, looking at inscriptions once sharply chiselled, now blurred by the passage of wind and rain.

HERE LIE INTERRED THE
MORTAL REMAINS OF MARNET
LINTON, DIED JULY 17TH
1837 AGED 16 YEARS . . .

> SACRED TO THE MEMORY OF
> VALENTINE GOODCHILD, WHO
> DEPARTED THIS LIFE THE
> 17TH DAY OF DEC'BER 1795 AGED
> 69 YEARS . . .

> HERE LYETH THE BODY OF
> CHRISTIAN GRAHAME, RELICT
> OF ROBERT JARDYNE OF
> HOWLETTS FARM, DIED THE
> 1ST DAY OF JANUARY 1793 IN THE
> 90TH YEAR OF HER AGE. ASLEEP
> IN JESUS.

With a sudden stab of excitement, Anne recognized these names, not only 'Jardyne', but also 'Christian' and 'Robert'. She had forgotten, but now remembered, that they too had been mentioned on the flyleaf of the Bible. Robert had been Alice's twin brother. With sharpened eyes and mind, Anne went searching among the stones.

As Ben had told her, the churchyard was full of Jardynes, or Jardines, as the name seemed to have been spelt from the end of the eighteenth century. There was a Euphan Jardyne, who, Anne now remembered, had been Alice's father; it was just possible to read on his rain-pitted headstone that he had died of typhoid fever in 1733. There were Andrews and Deborahs and Elizabeths and Johns, some of whom had died as children, and some of whom had lived into ripe old age. In a shady corner by the gate, in an enclosure surrounded by a low parapet, some nineteenth-century Jardines, apparently the last to be buried here, lay in the shadow of an ornate marble memorial. Reflecting that the Jardines had become rather grander with the passing of time, Anne read the inscription.

> IN PROUD AND LOVING
> MEMORY OF CAPTAIN THE HON.
> JOHN HERRIES JARDINE,
> 1ST BATTALION, SCOTS GUARDS,

BORN 11TH MAY 1826, DIED OF
WOUNDS SUSTAINED AT THE
BATTLE OF INKERMAN,
5TH NOVEMBER 1854. THEIR
BODIES ARE BURIED IN PEACE,
BUT THEIR NAME LIVETH FOR
EVERMORE.

Which was doubtless what the Jardines who had raised the memorial had believed, thought Anne. For how could they possibly have imagined that exactly a century later, a great flood would cover their bodies, and wipe out their names until the end of time? But the flood would not cover the name of Alice Jardyne, who had been blotted out of the Book of Life. Search as she might among the windy grass, Anne could not find her memorial anywhere there.

8

The *Book of Deer*

Longing as she was to open it, Anne had no opportunity that evening to study the book which Mr Russell had lent her. When she approached the house, she was displeased to see a large green Humber Hawk parked in the lane outside, dwarfing Dr Farrar's black Morris Minor, and making it look even shabbier than usual. She knew that it belonged to Tudor and Margaret Hoggett, old university colleagues of her parents, whose daughter, Kathleen, had been Head Girl at her London school. One of the few things Jenny and Anne agreed about was disliking Kathleen Hoggett, and when Anne found her in the kitchen, sipping tea and looking like Marilyn Monroe come straight from Marks and Spencer, it spoiled what had been, until then, a rather pleasant day.

But Mrs Farrar, for all her apparent vagueness, was a stickler for good manners, so Anne smiled, and shook hands, and tried to look delighted that the Hoggetts, on a touring holiday over Easter, had that morning had the bright idea of dropping in on the Farrars.

'Just wanted to ask how the dig was coming along. Thought we'd have a squint. Hear you've found a skeleton,' barked Tudor, who always gave the impression of a man far too busy to waste time on pronouns. 'Wouldn't mind a guided tour before supper, Sarah.'

Which was how the Farrars discovered that the Hoggetts had dropped in for their evening meal. There was one egg per Farrar in the pantry.

The last of the guided tour party to leave the kitchen was Mrs Farrar, who hissed the order, 'Jenny, do something,' as she went. Panic quite spoiled for Jenny the sight of

Kathleen tottering across the cobbled yard in her high-heeled shoes, while the wind whipped her carefully arranged blonde hair into a small haystack.

Being Jenny, however, she managed to convert four eggs, a lump of Cheddar and a stale loaf into a delicious baked pudding, while Anne laid the table, and gave her a running commentary on Kathleen's progress round the excavations.

'She's got Ben in tow now,' she announced, peering through the tiny panes of the kitchen window. 'She's simpering, and giggling at something he's said. But I say, Jen—isn't she getting fat?'

'That isn't fat, Anne. That's sex appeal,' replied Jenny heavily, dropping a saucepan into the sink from a great height.

As she counted out forks and knives, Anne looked sideways at her sister's flushed face. It came as a surprise to her to realize that Jenny might be serious about Ben. He was dark, but he was neither tall nor handsome, and Anne had always supposed him to be but a pale understudy for Gregory Peck. But, she observed, it was not only the notorious Hitler Hoggett, former terror of the first-form cloakroom, who had changed. Jenny, although her mother would never have allowed her to wear the tight white sweater and black pencil skirt which Kathleen had on, was also becoming more woman-like. It was not so obvious when her shape was concealed by her pleated gym tunic, but when she was wearing her weekend clothes, the difference in her was marked. She had taken to wearing a string of pearl beads with her pink angora jumper, and nylon stockings instead of ankle socks. And with her carefully curled red hair combed into a passable imitation of the style favoured by the Queen's younger sister, and her small, bow-shaped mouth coloured with Cutex *Shocking Pink* lipstick, she had an air of being ready, avid for the future. Anne recognized this without understanding it. For her, there still seemed to be a great gulf between the ordered, sheltered life she led now, and the life of a grown-up, which she neither feared nor craved.

But she hated Kathleen Hoggett, and during the interminable supper-time that followed, was hot with indignation on Jenny's behalf.

At long last, however, it was all over. The unfortunate Ben, who had been dragged back to supper, and forced to make polite conversation to Kathleen, under Jenny's displeased eye, had swallowed his cheese-and-egg pudding, and departed. Jenny and Anne had coped silently with a mountain of washing-up, and had been in bed for an hour when the sounds of departure floated up to them.

'Lovely to see you all . . . What a nice surprise . . .'

'Let's meet in London soon . . .'

'Such a delicious supper . . .'

'It was nothing, Margaret . . . Oh, not at all . . .'

'I wish they had all choked,' muttered Jenny, in the darkness.

The Register of Baptisms, Marriages and Burials in the Parish of Deer, which Mr Russell showed Anne next morning in the chilly little vestry behind the Church, told her little that she did not know already. The cloth-bound typescript, a transcription of the original, was easy to read, and Anne was sure that she had not missed anything important. The baptism of Alice and her brother was recorded, *Februare 27 anno domini 1701, Robert and Alyse, twins, of Euphan and Janet Jardyne, of Howletts Farm, Dere.* It seemed that in those days, people had spelt as they felt inclined. Further on, she found the record of the marriage in 1722 of Robert and Christian Grahame, she who had lived to be nearly ninety, and was now asleep in Jesus. There was no mention in the likely years of a marriage for Alice. Robert and Christian had had five sons baptized between 1723 and 1731, and had buried two of them. Robert had died in 1739. There was no entry in 1726 recording the death of Alice, *blottit owt of the Boke of Lyffe.*

Anne copied into a notebook the words recording Alice's baptism, and walked home again, reflecting sadly that she still knew next to nothing for which there was any historical evidence. Later in the day, however, that was to change.

In the afternoon, Jenny went off on her bicycle through the hills to Kirkcudbright, to have her hair cut. In the unexpected peace which followed her departure, Anne took *A Book of Deer* into the kitchen, and settled down with it in a chair by the fire.

The book was, as Mr Russell had said, fascinating stuff, an anthology of life in the Valley from earliest times. It began with a chapter on the Stone Age cairns and stone circles which dotted the area, and there was a dark photograph of the Grey Mound thirty years before, sheltering its secret occupant under a hat of turf. There were extracts from old documents, which Anne found heavy-going, but most of the book was a pleasant hotch-potch of memories and anecdotes, verses, spells, old recipes and bits of folklore. The name 'Jardyne' cropped up here and there. One Tam Jardyne had been hanged for sheep-stealing in 1563, a 'Jardyne of Netherby' had been a notorious smuggler, while another, improbably called Jordan Ezekiel, had been Minister at Deer in the 1670s. But the book was 503 pages long, and after two hours, although she had had a very entertaining read, Anne was no nearer discovering anything she really wanted to know. So, because time was passing, and all too soon Jenny would come tumbling in, she decided that she must have a method. The book had no index, but was arranged, more or less, in chronological order. Tearing two strips from the edge of the morning newspaper, she slipped them into the book, one at page 300, and one at page 370. These pages covered the years between 1680 and 1745. She would read them carefully; there seemed little point in concentrating on anything else.

And that was how Anne came upon the name she was looking for, but had not really believed she would find, and, as she read, her mind was filled again with distress, and terror for the fate of a woman who had died two hundred and fourteen years before she was born.

The fanaticism of the seventeenth century seems incredible to the modern mind, but cannot be doubted, in view of the savage treatment of countless poor women accused of witchcraft during the years between 1600 and the second decade of the eighteenth century. From the Parish of Deer alone, we know the names of Jean Comenes, Agnes McKendrigg, Elspet Murdoch, Janet Gowane, Alys Jardyne and Margaret Buchan, all accused during this period.

That was all. The article was not about witches, but about the religious quarrels of the time, and the next paragraph was about something else. No details. Only the statement that Alice Jardyne had been accused as a witch.

Anne could not eat her supper that evening, and her mother said she hoped she was not catching measles, which had been rife at Marymount at the end of last term.

9

An Unwanted Part

Not surprisingly, Anne slept very badly that night. She did not know a great deal about witchcraft, and what it meant, beyond the fact that real witches had not advertised themselves by carrying broomsticks and wearing funny hats. She knew, vaguely, that witches were supposed to have sold their souls to the Devil, in exchange for magical powers, but regarded such an idea as nonsensical—oddly, perhaps, for a person who had so easily accepted the power of a magic stone. But what distressed her, and made her afraid for Alice Jardyne, was knowing that, long ago, belief in witchcraft had been part of everyday life.

The previous autumn, soon after their arrival in Scotland, Anne had gone with her father to visit Edinburgh Castle. When they were leaving, she had been intrigued to see a bronze fountain at the end of the Esplanade, which her father had told her was called the Witches' Well. On it, framed in a strange design of snake and foxgloves, were two women's faces, one beautiful and good, the other ugly and evil. This was a memorial, said the inscription on a plaque above, to many women, 'some evil, some misunderstood', who had been burned to death as witches near that spot. And, as she writhed, hot and worried in the darkness, Anne remembered something else that her father had told her. During the years between 1590 and 1725, around four thousand people had been tortured, tried and executed as witches in Scotland—one of the worst totals in Europe. Had Alice Jardyne been one of these? Had she been evil, or misunderstood? For even if witches had not really had the power to harm their neighbours, their intentions might have been evil. And why, Anne wondered despairingly, did it matter to her so much that Alice Jardyne should have been good? Was she herself bewitched by the cold charm-stone, which had made her see this girl, running barefoot through Hoolets' Wood, in peril of her life?

At eight o'clock, Anne got up feeling headachy, and as if she had gravel in her eyes. The last thing in the world she wanted to do was to go to the casting of the Deer Pageant in the Church Hall, but she had persuaded Jenny to come with her, and felt she could not possibly back out now. The poster in the window of Deer Post Office and General Store had invited them to turn up at half-past ten, so they did, and joined a crowd of about forty others, a few adults, but mostly young people on holiday from school, like themselves. There were more girls than boys, and more villagers than outsiders, which was what you were called if you hadn't lived in the Valley since Robert the Bruce hid out in the heather. Everyone hung about with an air of boredom, shoulders hunched and hands thrust into the pockets of school blazers worn over holiday clothes, grouping themselves with those they knew, and watching everybody else with mild hostility. No one spoke to Jenny and Anne, the arch-outsiders; they stood together in a corner of the dismal hall, eyeing with disfavour their fellow Thespians, and the lurid depictions of the Parables of Jesus on the walls.

'I don't know that this was a good idea, Anne,' remarked Jenny.

'No, it wasn't. Let's go,' replied Anne.

But it was too late. Before they could squeeze their way round the edge of the room, and get to the door, the way out was blocked by the producer, Mrs Russell, on her way in. A large, tweed-girt woman with a frizzy perm and a white smile, she shut the door purposefully behind her, ranks parted respectfully to let her through, and she progressed down the middle of the hall, calling out greetings as she went. 'Lovely to see so many of you. Good morning, Mrs Moodie. Nice to have you, Miss Clow. Three Brodies, have we? My goodness! And the Farrar girls! Wonders will never cease!'

45

'Damnation,' muttered Jenny, sorely provoked. But both she and Anne accepted that escape was impossible now.

Mrs Russell, who was carrying a sheaf of papers and a large notebook, mounted a platform at the end of the hall, and sat down, overlapping a small chair.

'Find yourselves a pew, everyone,' she invited, and there was much scraping and banging as folding wooden chairs were seized from a stack by the door, and set down in a rough semicircle around the base of the platform. When they were all seated, Mrs Russell launched herself on a tide of enthusiasm.

The Pageant, she told them, would be performed in the School Field on the afternoon of Saturday the twenty-third of June. There would be a wooden stage, and a covered stand would be erected for the benefit of five-shilling and half-crown ticket holders. The less affluent could brave the elements on uncovered benches for a shilling. Children would be half-price. Mr Maxton had kindly offered the use of two marquees; one would be used as a dressing-room, and in the other the ladies of the Women's Guild would serve afternoon teas.

'And now, to the Pageant itself. My husband has written us a splendid script,' Mrs Russell told her audience proudly, 'and we must all try to do justice to it, mustn't we? There will be seven scenes, each telling part of the history of our little Valley, and these will be linked by interludes, about which I'll tell you presently. Just before we read for parts, though, let me ask you one or two questions which will help me to get things sorted out. How many of you girls have had dancing lessons?' Anne, along with half a dozen others, raised her hand, and Mrs Russell wrote down their names in her notebook. 'How many of you can sing on your own?'

There was no enthusiasm at all for this. Jenny nudged Anne, who sang beautifully, several times, and, when Anne failed to respond, said loudly, 'Anne can, Mrs Russell.'

'What? Anne can? Splendid! Of course you will, Anne, won't you? Mustn't hide your light under a bushel, dear.'

46

And before Anne could agree or protest, her name had been written down in a column by itself.

'You're a pig, Jen,' she said.

'Yes, I know,' replied Jenny calmly.

Then the reading for parts began. One by one, people were called out, and asked to read a speech. This seemed merely a formality, as no one, no matter how badly they read, failed to get the part. The Manse girls, Mary, Dorcas and Rachel, were all unblushingly allocated starring roles by their mother, and the only other major female part, rather to Anne's chagrin, was given to Jenny. Mrs Russell said that they needed someone with nice red hair to play the part of Mary, Queen of Scots, who had apparently spent her last night in Scotland at nearby Dundrennan Abbey, before fleeing over the Border into England. Anne thought crossly how much better she would herself have been in the part, and wanted to ask Mrs Russell if she had ever heard of a theatrical wig. Her headache was really bad now, and when she realized that Mrs Russell was casting the one-line and walk-on parts, and her name still hadn't been called, she felt humiliated, and close to tears. But there was worse to come.

Having cast the plays, Mrs Russell turned her attention to the interludes, which, she said, were to be 'little bits of fun', in contrast with the more serious historical scenes. Three were to be presented by what Mrs Russell called 'professionals', acrobats from Hailey's Circus, young soldiers from the Cameronian Regiment, the Pipe Band from St Ninian's Boys' School. 'But the other two we shall be putting on ourselves,' she announced cheerfully. 'In one, the wee folk from the village school will be performing some little dances and singing games of yester-year, while in the other we're going to have a Dance of Witches, which is where you singing and dancing girls come in. The Valley was once quite famous for its witches, my husband tells me. Won't that be fun?'

Which was how Anne discovered that she was destined to take part in some tomfool caper with broomsticks and steeple hats, at a time when she was desperately and

47

hopelessly trying to banish witchcraft from her mind.

At lunch, Jenny, who hadn't particularly wanted to take part in the Pageant at all, was all delight over her part, which would give her the opportunity to dress up like a peacock, and show off in an imperious fashion. She said over and over again that she could scarcely believe her good luck, and speculated gloatingly about the magnificence of the costume she would have to wear. Tact was not a conspicuous virtue in Jenny. Anne, who was doing her best to swallow spoonfuls of glutinous Heinz' Scotch Broth, and not succeeding very well, quickly tired of her sister's voice. 'Well, I've changed my mind,' she said peevishly. 'I don't want to take part after all, and I'm not going back. You can tell Mrs Russell, Jenny.'

But she might have known that her mother would never permit this.

'I'm sorry, Anne, but I think you must go back. This was your idea, and just because Jenny has got a better part than you, you've no reason to be a bad sport, and let Mrs Russell down. If you're the only person who can sing, she really is going to need you. You must go again with Jenny on Friday.'

Anne's eyes filled with tears, but she belonged to a generation which did not question parental authority, and she knew that that was that.

When they got up from the table, however, Mrs Farrar came to Anne, looked at her closely, and put a cool hand on her forehead.

'You're not well, my chicken,' she said. 'I wonder if it's measles, after all. Go upstairs and get into bed, and I'll bring you up a hot-water bottle, and an aspirin. Does your head ache, darling?'

Anne said that it did. She was thankful to undress, and climb into the high, old-fashioned bed, but when her mother came upstairs with the hot-water bottle, she said guiltily, 'I'm sorry, Mother. I know you have more important things to do.'

'I have nothing in the world more important to do,' replied Mrs Farrar firmly, as she lifted the covers, and slipped in the hot bottle at Anne's feet. When she had given her the aspirin, she sat down on the bed, and said, 'I'm not sure whether you can have measles twice. You have had it, quite badly, when you were little.'

'I know,' said Anne. 'I don't think it's measles.'

'Is something worrying you, my love?'

'I don't want to be a witch,' said Anne.

Mrs Farrar's austere face softened indulgently at what she obviously saw as a piece of sheer childishness.

'Don't want to be a witch?' she repeated. 'Well, it isn't the part I'd have chosen for you myself—you're far too pretty. But then, I may be partial. Anyway, why not just treat the whole thing as a joke? It doesn't matter very much, does it? And Daddy and I will be so proud to hear you sing. Now, try to go to sleep. Jenny will make something nice for your supper, although I'm afraid that being a queen may have a bad effect on her cooking. I'm going next door to play with my bones, so call if you need me.'

She got up and went to the door, but as she was opening it, Anne called her back.

'Mother.'

'Yes, what is it?'

'I was thinking. I know you're not the run-of-the-mill Marymount Mummy, but I love you.'

Mrs Farrar laughed.

'Do you, now?' she said. 'Well, that's good to know. I realize I must be an awful embarrassment most of the time.'

Anne was asleep almost before she closed the door.

10

At Another Address

Comforted by her mother's nearness, Anne slept dreamlessly until evening. At seven o'clock, Jenny brought her a plate of her favourite macaroni cheese; when she had eaten it she had a bath and returned to bed. She did not even hear Jenny coming to join her at half-past nine, but slept on until morning. Then, since no spots had appeared, Mrs Farrar said she could get up. She still felt troubled about Alice Jardyne, and lonely because she could not share her anxiety with anyone else, but because she had slept properly, she was better able to cope.

That afternoon, in the cool April sunshine, she walked with her mother and Jenny up through Hoolets' Wood to the Witch's Cottage, a roofless, burnt-out stone shell tucked into a sheltering flap of hillside, just below the summit of Cairnshee. Although many years must have passed since it was inhabited, one could still discern around it the ghost of a garden, with seeded snowdrops and wild garlic growing among the roots of thin, leggy roses, and rowan saplings which had forced their way up through a hawthorn hedge. So many things named after witches, Anne reflected now—this cottage, the bridge over the Water of Deer, the deep pool upstream from it which was called the Witch's Dam. She had never thought about it before, but, remembering what she had read yesterday in Mr Russell's book, it did seem that the Valley might have been famous for its witches, long ago.

And it was impossible not to wonder how many of these places were associated with Alice Jardyne, who might have been evil, or only misunderstood. Of course the Cottage might have been tenanted by Jean Comenes, or Janet

Gowane, or Elspet Murdoch—but Anne could not help wondering whether the snowdrops, and the frail primroses under the ruined wall, were descendants of those once planted here by Alice Jardyne. Jenny picked a few pallid daffodils for the kitchen table, and they walked down another way, over moors beyond which they caught glimpses of dark grey sea.

On Friday, because she had to, Anne went back to the Church Hall with Jenny, for the first Pageant rehearsal. Jenny, who was evidently to receive star treatment, was given her part to learn, and asked civilly to come on Tuesdays and Thursdays, at five o'clock, without fail. 'For we shall all be counting on you, dear, shan't we?' But Anne was told by Mrs Russell, already sighing audibly under the strain of her task, that, for the moment, she need only memorize her song. 'Miss Groom from the Schoolhouse is attending to the choreography, dear, and she'll let you know when she needs you. I'm going to be overworked as it is, just dealing with the drama side of things.'

'Yes, all right, Mrs Russell,' said Anne, hoping she didn't sound too pleased. She rather liked Miss Groom, a tall, dryly humorous woman who was the village schoolmistress. But she did seem an unlikely choreographer, and as Anne put the song-sheet into her blazer pocket, she couldn't help wondering what kind of choreography was required for a dance of witches. She had imagined a silly romp, with everyone inventing their own steps around a cauldron, but now she had a vision of some high-heeled, leg-kicking line-up, like the Television Toppers in steeple hats. She still hated the idea of dressing up as a witch, but, momentarily, she was inclined to laugh.

All too soon the Easter holiday was over, and the next week, as the last April of the Valley thickened and whitened into May, Jenny and Anne went back to school.

'My last term,' said Jenny, with real regret, as she laid

out her grey gym tunic and red blouse, ready for the first day of term. She had complained endlessly about the hideousness of grey lisle-thread stockings, and the indignity of pink elastic suspenders and navy-blue knickers, yet now she felt quite sentimental about them.

'I just wish it was my last,' sighed Anne, who was reluctantly sewing a new red ribbon round the crown of a battered grey felt hat. And as she said it, the thought of the future swept over her like a black wave.

Ever since they had come to Deer, Anne had longed to be one of the cheerful, casual, hatless crowd who packed the school bus as far as Kirkcudbright, where the local Academy was. From the beginning, she had hated Marymount School, although, initially, she had accepted her parents' reasoning that she and Jenny had better go to a school which would prepare them for English, rather than Scottish, examinations. And she had consoled herself with the thought that it was only for one year. But then, to her horror, after Christmas it had been decreed that she should return to Marymount, as a boarder, to complete her education, when her family had gone back to London. Anne had protested loudly, but, as usual, she had been gently overruled.

'It's an excellent school, Anne. Daddy and I are most impressed,' her mother had said, conveying the news. 'If you really want to go to Cambridge, you couldn't do better than to stay on there. We've talked to Miss McGill, and we're all agreed that another move at this stage wouldn't be a good idea.'

Anne did want to go to Cambridge, more than anything, but, 'I don't like Marymount. The food's awful,' she pointed out.

'We're not sending you there for the food, my love, we're sending you for the teaching. That isn't awful, as your exam results show.'

Too late, Anne wished she had made a mess of the exams.

'I'll get fat,' she threatened.

'Good,' replied Mrs Farrar approvingly.

Anne looked at the loving, unyielding face in exasperation. But she reckoned she held a trump card.

'It's supposed to be against your principles,' she reminded her mother sternly. 'You're always saying that a good state system of education, with equal opportunity for all, is the only hope for a decent society in the future.' She said it as one quoting word for word, as indeed she was.

'Well, yes,' agreed Mrs Farrar. 'So it is. But that doesn't mean that I want to sacrifice your best interest to a general principle. As a parent, I want you to have the best education available, and that will be obtained by keeping you at Marymount.'

Anne was shocked by this evidence of double standards, but she knew that she was beaten, and said no more.

So there was nothing for it but to accept the bracing, regimented life of Marymount, Latin verbs and mutton stew, quadratic equations and compulsory games, chapel and learning Shakespeare by heart. Anne got on with her work, and consoled herself with the dream of Cambridge, four years hence. Cambridge, where her mother had studied in the twenties, and where Anne would do the same. For her, that was the light at the end of the Marymount tunnel, and one day she would be as fine an archaeologist as her mother.

When she stepped back after Easter, however, into the unloved but familiar school world, Anne was not quite the same single-minded girl she had been last term. There was another exam hurdle to be cleared in June, and already she was revising with her usual thoroughness. But always, folded away at the back of her mind, was the memory of Alice Jardyne, accused of witchcraft, and blotted out of the Book of Life. That the witchcraft and the blotting out were connected, Anne had no doubt at all; what troubled her was the feeling that her investigations had reached a dead end. Rack her brains as she might, she could think of no one she could approach, no new book she might consult, which might tell her what she wanted to know. She knew there was no point in suggesting to her father that he might take her to Edinburgh, to the Scottish Record Office. He would simply say, 'Sorry, my dear. I'm far too busy.' He was still in thrall to the nameless skeleton-girl, about whom he knew even less than Anne knew about Alice Jardyne. Slowly, it was dawning on Anne that her parents were the sort of people who enjoyed philosophizing more than proof—and, even more slowly, that she might not herself be that sort of person at all.

In desperation, she took to crystal-gazing. She had gone on, day after day, wearing the charm-stone on the chain around her neck; she was not supposed to wear jewellery with her school uniform, but the stone hung neatly in the space between her tiny breasts, and the chain was hidden by the high collar of her blouse. It had not previously occurred to her that she might manipulate it, but now, convinced that it had worked a wonder once, she would take the thing out and turn it over furtively in her fingers, staring at its polished surface, willing it to show her something more. But to no avail. The stone lay cold and indifferent in her hand, mysterious only in its age and provenance.

Eventually, Anne tired of it. She did not forget Alice Jardyne, nor did she stop believing that it was important for her to find out the rest of her story. But school, homework and rehearsals with Miss Groom occupied her time, and nearly three weeks passed before, suddenly, the wheels of the mystery began to turn again.

On a bright Saturday morning, when there was no school, Anne was coming downstairs to breakfast. The front door was open, and, as she reached the hall, the postman rode up on his red bicycle. Without dismounting, he tossed a handful of letters on to the doormat. Anne picked them up, took them into the kitchen, and began to sort them out on the table.

'Two, boiled, please, Jen,' she said, and the long-suffering Jenny put the eggs into the pan.

Most of the letters were for Dr Farrar. Mrs Farrar had one from her sister in America, and Jenny one from a London friend. None of these interested Anne. The one which caught her attention was not addressed to a member of the Farrar family at all.

> Maj. John Berresford Jardine, M.C.,
> The Owls' House,
> Deer,
> Kirkcudbrightshire.

In sheer astonishment, Anne stared at the long buff envelope, with its purple threepenny stamp and typed direction. Then abruptly she lifted it, stalked across the hall, and knocked on the study door.

'Daddy,' she said unceremoniously, walking in without waiting to be asked, 'who on earth is Major John Berresford Jardine?'

Dr Farrar lowered the *Manchester Guardian*, and looked at Anne over his spectacles, too surprised to be annoyed.

'The chap who owns this house,' he said. 'Why?'

'There's a letter for him in the post.'

'Good lord!' exclaimed Dr Farrar. 'Is that so? He must have moved from here all of seven years ago. Leave it on the table, Anne, and I'll readdress it.'

Anne put the envelope on the table, but before she went, she said, 'Daddy—the day I found the Bible—why didn't you tell me the landlord's name was Jardine?'

'Eh? Should I have? Maybe I assumed you knew. Why?'

'He must be descended from the family in the Bible.'

'Well, yes. Obviously. Same house,' said Dr Farrar, who was never at his best in the morning.

Anne went away before her annoyance surfaced, and a ticking-off for rudeness ensued. When she had finished her breakfast, however, and was about to go upstairs to make the bed, she again encountered her father, this time in the hall. He was on his way out to the dig, and he had the letter in his hand.

'Anne,' he said. 'Be a love, and run along to the pillar-box with this, will you? If I leave it on the table, it will disappear under the litter, and I'll find it again in August.'

Anne knew that this was true. 'Yes, of course,' she said, taking the letter, and memorizing Major Berresford Jardine's new address at a glance.

> Maryfield House,
> Marywell,
> by Dunchree.

Thoughtfully, she put on her blazer, and walked along to the postbox at the end of the lane. By the time she got back, she had made up her mind what to do. She went straight upstairs, made the bed, yet again cleared Jenny's make-up off her desk, and sat down to write a letter.

> *The Owls' House,*
> *Deer.*
> *18 May 1954*

Dear Major Berresford Jardine,
> *At the end of March, I found a very old Bible in a hidden cupboard in my bedroom here. It had a lot of names in it, of people who must be your ancestors. I have become interested in one of them, a young woman called Alice Jardyne, who died in 1726. I have tried to find out about her, but have not had much success.*
> *I wondered if you could tell me anything about her. I don't mean to be nosy, but I am interested in history. I should be very grateful. Daddy is going to give you the Bible and the other things I found when he sees you.*

> *Yours sincerely,*
> *Anne Farrar*

It was an awful letter, stilted and boring, but it would have to do. You could scarcely tell a stranger that you knew his ancestress had been a witch, or that a magic stone had caused you to see her being hounded through a wood in her bare feet. As she addressed the envelope, and stuck on a stamp, Anne wondered what on earth had possessed an elderly gentleman—she assumed that ex-army officers were old—to leave the Owls' House for a place like Maryfield. She and Jenny passed it every day on their way to and from school, and Anne thought it was the most hideous house she had ever seen. On the landward side of the coast road, overlooking the Bay, it was a raw, flat-roofed, one-storeyed building of brashly modern design, set down amid flat green lawns ringed with trees which would take twenty years to grow up to a sheltering height. Whereas the Owls' House had a flower garden, and an orchard, and a rowan-tree at its gate.

Anne went to the postbox again, then settled down, as patiently as she could, to wait for a reply. She reckoned that the earliest one could possibly arrive was Wednesday, and she had to put in the time between as best she might. There was homework to be done, and on Monday and Tuesday, in the afternoons, she had rehearsals at the village school for the Witches' Dance. She had been relieved, at the first rehearsal, to discover that there were to be no steeple hats, and no cauldron. The witches were to wear long wigs, tartan plaids and tattered dresses, and the dance was to be a wild Scots reel, to the accompaniment of bagpipes played by Miss Groom's nephew, dressed as the Devil. Anne was to sing her song as the others skipped off at the end of the dance.

'Did witches dance?' Anne asked Miss Groom, as she helped her lock up the schoolroom, after Tuesday's rehearsal.

The schoolmistress gave her a dark-eyed, thoughtful look.

'I doubt it,' she said. Then, 'You don't like this very much, do you, Anne?'

Anne said honestly that it wasn't the role she would have chosen.

'No, nor would I,' agreed Miss Groom. 'I said at the Committee meeting that I thought it was in bad taste, but I'm afraid I was overruled—told that it was all harmless fun, and that no one remembered the reality of the witch-hunt nowadays, anyway. I didn't feel that was the point, but since I had already agreed to take charge of the music and dancing, there wasn't a lot I could do.'

She walked with Anne to the gate, along a path between the children's little garden-plots. As they reached the road, Anne said, 'Miss Groom, do you know who the witch was—the one that the Bridge and the Cottage are called after?'

Miss Groom shook her cropped grey head. 'No. I don't know anything at all about the Valley witches, Anne,' she said. 'But they did exist, and something tells me it's wrong to make entertainment out of unspeakable human suffering, even if it did take place three hundred years ago. That's why I put my foot down about the cauldron and the poky hats. I'm afraid Mrs Russell is less than pleased with me.'

Anne went home more than pleased with Miss Groom. But when she thought about it later that night, in bed, it occurred to her that—although Miss Groom had done her best—a boisterous dance to the music of a pantomime Devil was scarcely less insulting to the memory of tortured souls than a fairy-tale caper around a cauldron. Indeed, in a way, the fairy-tale version might have been easier to cope with because it was purely fantasy. The dance, with its ragged, jerking figures and mad music had just enough of reality in it to make it frightening . . . What Anne could not understand was why she felt so passionate about it. Unable to take her mother's well-intentioned advice to treat the whole thing as a joke, unable to shrug it off as a tasteless incident for which she was not responsible, she was aware that there was another element in her feeling about it. But, as yet, its true nature eluded her.

On Wednesday morning, the hoped-for letter arrived. It was written in uneven black writing, on thick cream paper.

Maryfield House,
by Dunchree.
22nd May

Dear Anne,
I have both bad and good news for you. The

58

*bad is that my husband has never heard of Alice
Jardyne, and can't imagine why anyone would
want to know about her. The good news is that I
have heard of her, and know a little, which I shall
be glad to share.*

*Can you come to tea on Saturday, about four
o'clock? Telephone (Dunchree 25) if you can't. If I
don't hear from you, I shall expect you.*

> *Yours sincerely,*
> *Joscelyn Jardine*

Anne kept this letter in her pocket, and reread it so often
that, by Friday, it had acquired quite a tattered look.

Her only problem was that she must ask her parents'
permission to go to Dunchree, which was twelve miles
away, on a Saturday. She had been so careful not to let
anyone know of her preoccupation with Alice Jardyne that
it could be awkward trying to explain her interest now.
Mrs Farrar might think she had been forward in writing a
letter to someone she didn't know, and might disapprove
of her intruding on Mrs Jardine.

But she need not have worried. By good fortune, on
Friday afternoon, Mrs Farrar had uncovered, in the
forecourt of the Grey Mound, a ritual fire-pit, containing
fragments of oak charcoal, and cremated human bones.
This altered in a flash the Farrars' theory regarding the age
and usage of the cairn; the presence of both cremated and
uncremated bones on the same site was so overwhelmingly
exciting, apparently, that they could concentrate on
nothing else.

'Just wait till Tudor Hoggett hears about this!' was the
glad cry. 'It blows all his theories to smithereens!'

'They're worse than children,' tutted Jenny disapprov-
ingly.

But the discovery was timely, for when Anne went to ask
her mother's leave to cycle over to Maryfield House next
day, Mrs Farrar merely looked up from her microscope,
momentarily wiped the gloating expression off her face,
and said, 'Of course, Anne. That will be nice for Mrs

Jardine. I don't suppose she meets many people.' Then she dropped her head over her work again.

Confirmed in her assumption that Mrs Jardine was a rheumaticky old lady, Anne went off to bed. After lunch next day she borrowed Jenny's bicycle and set off, pedalling doggedly into the wind.

11

A Significant Day

In most lives, there are a few days so significant that, afterwards, they are always recalled in their setting of weather. In the years to come, Anne would remember very clearly that airy cycle ride from Deer to Dunchree, light and shade shifting on the bare hills, the hundred different greens of the woods, clouds running and gulls drifting on the wind. For the first seven miles, the road wound up the Valley's side, in and out of spruce plantations, with heathery moorland between, but always there was salt on the wind, blowing from the unseen sea.

Then suddenly, over the Valley's brim, the sky was immensely tall, falling straight down into the shattered mirror of the Bay. Long before she reached it, Anne could see the Jardines' house beneath her, a vast white letter 'E' written in stone and concrete on the grass. Leisurely, after the long climb out of the Valley, she free-wheeled down the twisting road and, at five to four, arrived at white gates in a grey stone wall. The name, *Maryfield House*, was painted on the right-hand gate, which had been left open.

Anne dismounted, and pushed Jenny's bicycle along a smoothly-paved drive to a white front door. She propped the bicycle against the wall, and rang the bell. After the usual nerve-wracking pause, the door was opened by a woman in a green dress, broadly built and with dark hair going grey.

'You'll be Anne,' she said, fortunately just before Anne made the mistake of calling her 'Mrs Jardine'. 'Come in, my dear. Mrs Jardine is expecting you.'

Anne only had time to notice a wide, fawn-carpeted hall, empty of furniture apart from a table with flowers on it, and an umbrella-stand full of fishing-rods and shepherds' crooks. She followed the woman across the carpet to a door which slid sideways across the wall, heard her say, 'Your visitor has come, Mrs Jardine,' and found herself standing alone as the door rolled shut behind her. She saw another expanse of carpet, some dark antique furniture placed against pale blue walls, and an enormous window filled with sea. Sitting in front of the window was a woman who raised her head from a book, and looked at Anne. She seemed a long way away, so Anne walked towards her.

Mrs Jardine was not, after all, the old lady of Anne's imagining. Anne was hopeless at guessing people's ages, but she knew that she could not be more than thirty. She was also beautiful, in a thin, finely-drawn way, with wavy brown hair, simply cut, and slate-grey eyes which looked dark in the paleness of her face. She was wearing a plain white blouse, and no jewellery apart from her wedding ring and tiny gold studs in her ears. No pearl beads, no bright lipstick, yet she had the cool, modern look which Jenny longed to achieve, and which made Anne uncomfortably aware of her ill-fitting kilt, her spectacles, and her woollen ankle socks. But all the advantage was not on Mrs Jardine's side, and now Anne understood in a flash the peculiar flatness of the house and its garden. For she was sitting in a wheeled invalid chair, with a pillow at her back, and a pink blanket folded over legs so thin and flat that they didn't make any contours in its surface. Inevitably, there was a moment of constraint as they eyed each other, but then Mrs Jardine held out her hand, and said, 'Anne, how do you do? It's good of you to come to see me.'

Anne didn't see that it was good of her at all. She went and took the offered hand in hers, saying, 'No. It's good of you to see me. I didn't realize you were ill.'

The denial came quickly. 'I'm not. I had polio, seven years ago. I know it's difficult, but I'd be grateful if you'd pretend you didn't notice.'

Anne knew about polio. There was a 'scare' every summer, and in some years an epidemic. There were numbers of cases reported in the newspapers, uneasy parents, always some deaths—and, until very recently, no prospect of a cure. Now there was talk of a vaccine from America, but meanwhile, unlucky young people could be left—like this.

She said, 'Yes, of course. I'm sorry, Mrs Jardine.'

'Why not call me Polly?' was the reply.

Anne, after expecting a formal old lady, was pleased by this invitation, but surprised, too.

'I thought your name was Joscelyn,' she said.

For the first time, she saw that Polly Jardine had a very nice smile.

'So it is,' she agreed. 'I write it on letters, but no one ever calls me that, thank goodness.' She waved in the direction of a tea-tray which stood ready on a table by the stone fireplace, and went on, 'Now pour us some tea, please, and take the food beside you. You must eat as much as you can, because Mrs Armitage's dustbin of a dog will get the rest, and chocolate cake is bad for his teeth.'

'Was that Mrs Armitage who let me in?' asked Anne, as she poured tea from a silver pot into delicate china cups. 'I thought it was you. I imagined a Major's wife would be quite old.'

She could see that Polly was amused by this.

'I'm twenty-seven,' she replied frankly. 'You're thinking of a Major-General's wife, I expect—like my mother. Mrs Armitage keeps house for us, and helps Johnny to look after me.' She took the cup and saucer which Anne brought her, saw that she was settled in an armchair with a plate of chocolate cake beside her, then said, 'Now, Anne, please—tell me what this is all about. I've been consumed with curiosity ever since your letter arrived.'

So, between mouthfuls, Anne told her about the wall falling down, and the hidden cupboard, and the name in the Bible, and how appalled she had been by the words, *blottit owt of the Boke of Lyffe*. She explained how Ben had directed her to the Minister, who had given her the book which mentioned that Alice Jardyne had been accused of witchcraft. 'I suppose—now—that somebody thought she should be blotted out of the Book of Life because she was a witch,' she said, 'but I haven't been able to find out anything else.'

'I think,' said Polly Jardine, who had listened intently to Anne's account, 'you could assume that the person who wanted her blotted out of the Book of Life was the same person who accused her of witchcraft in the first place. Why do you want to know about this, Anne?'

The question came suddenly, and Anne was at a loss for a reply. She looked into the gravely questioning eyes, and shook her head. 'I don't know,' she said. 'It seems important. I don't know why.'

'Yes. Strange,' said Polly thoughtfully. 'It seems important to me, too.' She was silent for a moment, watching Anne making sure that the dustbin-dog had a poor supper, then she said, 'I don't know everything about this affair, Anne. Far from it. But I know more than you do, and I'll be glad to tell you—although I warn you, it isn't a pleasant story. I first came upon Alice Jardyne's name a long time ago. When we came here to live in 1948, I was going through a phase when I was even more ill-tempered and difficult than I am now, and poor Johnny was at his wits' end trying to find something that would interest me. He'd tried all sorts of things, and I couldn't be bothered with any of them. Then one night he came home with an old suitcase full of family papers, which he thought I might like to have a look at—I'd done a year of History at London University before we were married. I can't say I felt much enthusiasm, but he'd been all the way to his solicitor's office in Glasgow to fetch the papers on a filthy day, despite not being in the least interested himself. The only ancestor Johnny knows anything about was a Captain in the Guards who did dashing things in the Crimean War, and would have been court-martialled, my father says, if he hadn't got himself killed first. Besides, I was having a fit of being ashamed of the self-pitying, whining bore I'd become. So I said yes, I would look at them, and that was how I first encountered the name of Alice Jardyne. Most of the papers were legal—wills, and property transactions. But there were some private letters, and at the bottom of the case I found Alice's own Bible, her copy of *The Pilgrim's Progress*, and a manuscript book which was also hers.'

'Gosh! What was in it?' asked Anne, who was finding this story fascinating.

'All sorts of things,' Polly told her. 'Recipes, and accounts, and prayers, and quotations from the Bible. Some pen-and-ink drawings. Spells.'

'Spells?' repeated Anne, in surprise. 'Then she really was a witch?'

Polly made a circular gesture with long hands which, Anne noticed, were rarely still. 'Only in a sense,' she said. 'Alice was a country healer, at a time when medicine as we understand it was unknown. She practised what's called white witchcraft—herbalism, with a bit of harmless magic and religion mixed in. The Church, which was very powerful in Scotland, didn't approve, and never seems to have drawn any distinction between white witchcraft and the more sinister kind. But if people were desperate for cures, I don't suppose they were put off by the Minister's disapproval. Alice's mother was the local wise woman, quite famous for her healing skills, and she taught Alice. I got all the information I have about the family from some letters which were tucked in at the back of the book, which Alice had written to her sister Janet. Janet had married a farmer called Burnes, and had gone to live twenty miles away, up at Clatteringshaws.'

'Yes! That's in the Bible,' exclaimed Anne, remembering. 'Isaac Burnes of the Lea.'

'Yes,' agreed Polly. 'That's the man. I have the book here—' she pointed to the table which stood beside her chair '—and Alice's *Pilgrim's Progress* and Bible are in Johnny's office. I'm afraid the letters went back to Glasgow a long time ago.' She sat silent for a moment, looking at Anne with her pensive grey eyes. Then she shifted her position slightly by leaning on her hands, and went on, 'Alice Jardyne had a spinal deformity. She had a hump on her left shoulder, and a withered left arm. She was very well educated for a woman of her time, she was intelligent and compassionate, devoted to her family, fond of animals and her garden—a good and gentle creature. But she lived in a very superstitious age, and in an isolated, uncouth part of the world, where it was more than a disadvantage to be different from your neighbours—it was downright dangerous. Her mother died when she was fifteen, and after her sister's marriage in 1719, she kept house for her father and brother—'

'At the Owls' House?'

'Yes. It was called Hoolets' Farm at that time, which is a much nicer name, don't you think? Anyway, Alice kept the house until her brother married. That was when things began to go badly wrong for her. She and her twin, Robert, had always been close friends, and her new sister-in-law—called "Christian", of all unsuitable names—was violently jealous. She didn't rest until she'd got Alice out of the house, and banished to that little place up on the hill above Hoolets'—Cairnshee, isn't it?—that they call the Witch's Cottage. Do you know it, Anne? Johnny and I used to picnic in the garden there, in the days when that was still possible.'

Anne said, 'I've been there often. I wondered—who the witch was.'

'Yes. I didn't know at the time, either. Well, not content with having separated from her family a girl who really needed their care and protection, the unspeakable Christian then had to go whispering among the neighbours about a withered arm being the Devil's mark, and stirring up their superstitious fears with talk of the Evil Eye. It wasn't long before they were afraid to go to Alice for help if they were ill, and if she came into the village, the children threw stones and the adults set their dogs on her.'

Anne's eyes met Polly's in a glance of horrified sympathy.

'But she had a father, and a brother,' she whispered. 'Didn't they try to protect her?'

'No,' Polly said. 'Her father was sick and prematurely aged, and as for Robert—I think he did care for Alice up to a point, but he had a very weak character. He was afraid of his wife, and of public opinion, and I suppose he was afraid of witchcraft too. Anyway, in the year 1725, Christian had the final piece of luck she'd been hoping for. There had been a bad outbreak of murrain—cattle-fever—in the Valley, and the animals were dying by the score. It was a disaster for the whole community, and a scapegoat was needed. It wasn't difficult for Christian to persuade her cronies that the hunchbacked, solitary Alice was casting evil spells. A dozen of them went to the Minister, and a charge of witchcraft was brought before the Kirk Session. It's all in the last letter Alice wrote to her sister, the most painful document I've ever read in my life.'

'What happened then?' asked Anne, sensing uncomfortably that she was in the presence of someone who grieved for Alice Jardyne even more than she did herself.

'I don't know, Anne,' Polly said. 'At the end of the last letter, Alice told her sister that she expected to be arrested, and taken to the Tolbooth in Kirkcudbright to await trial by the Civil Courts. She said she was afraid of what they would do to her, and I've been afraid too, ever since. But I don't know any more. I told you I only knew part of the story, and I'm afraid I'm not able to research the rest.'

Polly sat for a moment fingering the edge of her blanket, and looking at Anne, then she said, 'It's strange to find that you're interested in this too. I don't quite understand. For me, it's different. She was a cripple too, and I think sometimes that she would understand how tired and frustrated and cross I feel. But you're young and strong, and you have a good life ahead of you. Why should it matter to you?'

There was only one way to answer this, and, knowing instinctively that Polly Jardine would not laugh or tease her, Anne did what she had never thought she could do. Leaning forward, and resting her chin on her fist, she told someone else about her dream, and the mysterious finding of the charm-stone in the Grey Mound, and what she believed it had revealed to her in Hoolets' Wood. She took the charm-stone from her neck, and put it into Polly's hand; she saw her examine it with interest, but she knew before Polly spoke that any hope of enlisting her as a fellow believer was doomed to disappointment.

'You don't believe me, do you?' she asked sadly.

Polly answered carefully.

'I know you're telling me the truth, as it appears to you. And of course it explains your interest in Alice Jardyne. I agree that the dream was very strange, and it did show something which might have happened to her, although God forbid that it did. But I'm not going to say that I believe magic stones can exert any real influence, Anne. That would be dishonest, and a bad beginning. We should start by being honest with each other, don't you think?'

Start what, Anne wondered. She thought she had only come to tea. But there was nothing in this gentle answer to make her feel hurt.

'It doesn't matter,' she said, and was about to add that she should be starting back, when something unexpected happened. In one of the dramatic changes in the weather which occurred in that part of the country, a flash of lightning illuminated the room. Almost simultaneously, thunder growled, and the sun vanished. While they talked, unseen bales of black cloud had come over the hills behind the house, and now whipped themselves flat across the sea. A grey curtain blotted out the Bay, and a gust of wind sent rain hurtling like gravel against the plate-glass window. Polly looked at Anne in dismay.

'Oh, dear,' she said. 'I hope your father's coming to fetch you?'

Anne explained that she had to cycle back. 'But don't worry, Polly,' she said soothingly. 'It will clear soon.'

'No, I'm afraid it won't,' said Polly, frowning. 'I know this weather. The thunder won't last, but it will rain until past midnight.' She thought for a moment, then added, 'Never mind. You can stay here tonight. I'll telephone your mother.'

'You can't,' Anne reminded her. 'No telephone.'

'Of course not. Silly of me. I know what, though,' replied Polly, brightening. 'I'll ask Mrs Armitage to send her son Steven over to the Owls' House on his motorcycle with a message, when the thunderstorm is past. He roars about the countryside in all weathers.'

'Couldn't I go with him?' suggested Anne, reluctant to be a nuisance.

'Certainly not. Much too dangerous,' said Polly. 'I suppose Johnny could run you back, but he may be very late tonight, and I'd rather he didn't have to turn out again. Besides, by that time your parents would be more than worried. So it will be easier if you stay. You will, won't you? Please?'

From this speech, Anne learned two things. First, that Polly really wanted her to stay. And second, that she was used to getting what she wanted.

'If you're sure it's all right, I'd like to stay,' she said.

'Good,' said Polly, with satisfaction. 'You can have Alice's book to read in bed.'

12

Alice's Book

So, instead of cycling home in the rain, Anne spent the evening in an unexpected, but pleasant way. Mrs Armitage said that Steven could easily run over to the Owls' House, and, after she had lit the fire and lifted Polly on to the sofa, she brought them a supper of salad and fruit on two trays. Then Anne, sensing that the telling of her story had tired Polly, and perhaps for the first time ever drawn out of self-absorption by the need of someone else, set about entertaining her.

She told her about life at the Owls' House in its crazier moments, about the skeleton in Jenny's bedroom, and Heinz' Three Varieties, and gave a demonstration of what had happened the day Mrs Farrar had accidentally stepped on a roller-skate, and discovered that she could turn a better cartwheel than she had ever imagined. Then she described Marymount, and gave spirited imitations of the Misses McGill, who owned the school, and were known collectively as the Weird Sisters. Individually they were known as the Tank, the Spitfire and the Jeep. They did not talk about Alice Jardyne again, but after Anne had told Polly about the Pageant, and imitated Jenny forgetting her lines while acting regally as Mary, Queen of Scots, she went on to talk of the Witches' Dance, and the song she was to sing.

'I hate the whole idea,' she admitted, 'but I have to go through with it now, for Miss Groom's sake. She's done her best, although she thinks it's in poor taste too.'

'Yes, I'm sure she does,' said Polly. 'I remember Miss Groom. I was engaged to Johnny in the last year of the war, and when he was on leave we stayed with his family at the Owls' House. We talked to her sometimes when we passed her garden. A nice woman.'

'Very,' agreed Anne.

Then suddenly, 'I want to hear the song,' demanded Polly, who was obviously enjoying her entertainment. 'Sing to me, Anne.'

'Oh, no. I couldn't,' replied Anne, feeling shy for no reason.

'Yes, you could. You've been an acrobat, and a mimic—now sing. Oh, go on, Anne, *please*.'

So, a little pink, but swallowing most of her embarrassment, Anne sang in her clear, treble voice.

'When the grey owl has three times hooed,
When the grimy cat has three times mewed,
When the fox has yowled three times in the wud
At the red mune cowrin' ahint the clud,
When the stars has cruppen deep i' the drift,
Lest cantrips pyke them oot o' the lift,
    Up, horses a', but mair adowe!
    Ride, ride to Lochar-brig-knowe!'

Polly enjoyed this so much that she made Anne sing it all over again. But when Anne had finished the second time, Polly looked at her seriously, and said, 'It makes it sound fun, doesn't it? The stars creeping under the clouds, scared of being picked out of the sky by magic spells, and witches riding off to have a merry time at their local coven. But whatever it was like, Anne, it wasn't like that. Maybe there were some covens, I suppose—but most witches were solitary, friendless people, picked out and lied about for things that were their misfortune, not their fault.' A dark, hurt expression showed in her tired eyes, and her voice dropped as she added, 'That's what I find most horrifying —they were tortured and killed for crimes which only existed in the imagination of other people. There's no defence against evil minds and mass hysteria, in any age.'

Anne decided quickly that it would be wise to change the subject, and began to tell a story based on Ben's futile effort to be charming to Jenny and to Kathleen Hoggett at the same time. She was relieved to see Polly smile, and relax again.

Not long afterwards, a small gold clock on the chimney-piece struck nine, and just after that a car turned into the drive from the road, the brightness of its headlamps momentarily splintering on the wet window. A few minutes later, the door opened, and John Jardine came into the room. He was a very tall, fair young man, with pale blue eyes in a hard, weather-beaten face which softened when he looked at his wife. Anne remembered what her father had said about him milking the cows with kid gloves on, and reckoned that this had been unfair. However rich he was, the large hand which he took out of his breeches pocket to shake hers was obviously used to hard work, ungloved.

'I heard your visitor was staying the night,' he said to Polly, then, giving her a keen look, 'You're tired, my girl.'

'No, I'm not,' said Polly, defiant, but quite unable to disguise her pleasure that he had come. 'I've had a lovely time, honestly.'

'Well, I'm glad, but you're coming to bed now. I'll show Anne the guest-room, then I'll come back and fetch you.'

Polly did not argue with this. She smiled at Anne, and said, 'I'll ask Mrs Armitage to bring your breakfast at half-past eight, but get up when you like. Sleep well, and thank you for amusing me. I don't know when I had such a pleasant evening. Alice's book is on the table by the window, Anne.'

Anne said good-night, fetched the leather-bound book, and went with Major Jardine across the hall to another door which opened sideways, so as not to impede a wheel-chair.

'Mrs A. will have left you everything you need, I think,' he said. 'Thank you for making Polly happy.'

To her annoyance, Anne felt herself blushing slightly.

'I hope she isn't too tired because of me,' she said awkwardly. She had had no experience of invalids, and wondered whether, in her desire to be entertaining, she had gone too far.

72

'Oh, it doesn't do her any harm to be tired by company,' Polly's husband told her. 'She's tired by being alone, too much of the time.'

To someone used to the Spartan conditions of the Owls' House, a night spent in the Jardines' guest-room was the last word in luxury. Dr and Mrs Farrar, although they liked a fire in their study and cushioned chairs at the end of the day, did not care about comfort generally, and ascribed the fall of the Roman Empire, in part at least, to the Romans' fondness for central heating. At home in St. John's Wood, their children associated warmth in the bedroom with being ill, and luxury in the bathroom was confined to an old cork bathmat. Anne, who had already decided that the Jardines' house was much nicer inside than outside, found the cosy, flowery-pink room very much to her taste. Mrs Armitage had turned down one of the twin beds, and had laid on it the most elegant silk nightdress that Anne had ever seen. When, tentatively opening a door, she found a tiled bathroom complete with expensive soap, bath salts and even a toothbrush, she began to feel that the thunderstorm had been a real stroke of luck. In the course of a long, fragrant bath, she decided to have her hair cut like Polly's, and to save up her meagre pocket-money until she had enough to buy a beautifully cut, elegantly simple, horribly expensive white blouse. Then she dried herself on a thick towel, put on the silk nightdress, and climbed into bed, opening at last the book which had belonged to Alice Jardyne.

It was a long, narrow manuscript book with thick yellow pages, the black writing very clear because it had never been exposed to the light. Alice had written her name inside the cover of the book, *Alyce Jardyne*; her handwriting was cramped and ornately looped, but quite easy to read. Thrilled, yet awed to be handling a book which Alice Jardyne had touched, Anne turned the pages slowly, reading first the recipes for cooking food. *Receipt*

for broyld eels. Receipt for fricasy of rabits with mush-rom sauc. To rost ane turkie. To baik ane pigion py.
There were household accounts in this first section of the book too. In January 1719, Alice had paid twelve shillings for *a floorisht hood and apron*; in November 1721 she had bought *2 pr threed stockins, 4 snuff handkerchieffs, 3 yds gingdum for a goun*, for nineteen shillings and five pence. When she remembered her vision of this girl, running barefoot in the wood dressed in filthy rags, Anne found this reading painful. Quickly she turned over the next few pages, which contained verses of the Bible, carefully copied, and found herself looking down at a double-spread of pen-and-ink drawings, the subject of which she instantly recognized.

When Anne and Jenny had been younger, in the late 1940s, they had spent their summer holidays in Yorkshire, at the home of their maternal grandmother, the widow of a Methodist clergyman. The tedium of stuffy, clove-scented Sundays in old Mrs Haldane's house was a memory they would carry with them always; everything was forbidden, it seemed, except for chapel in the morning and the evening, and dozing in the parlour in the afternoon. Normal reading was not permitted, but the two little girls were allowed two books, Arthur Mee's *Children's Bible*, and John Bunyan's *The Pilgrim's Progress*, to keep them quiet while their elders slumbered. Jenny had always preferred a surreptitious game of Patience behind the red plush sofa, but Anne had settled for *The Pilgrim's Progress*, and now, as she looked down at Alice's strangely animated drawings, it was as if she were meeting old acquaintances once again.

There were Giant Despair and Mercy and Christiana, and the characters Anne had called 'the Misters', Great-heart, and Worldly-wiseman, and Valiant-for-truth. And there, three times as large as any of them, was the foul Fiend Apollyon, with his scales like a fish, wings like a dragon, feet like a bear, and the mouth of a lion. As a small child, Anne had seen this menacing creature in nightmares, coming across the field towards her, as he had towards the

74

Pilgrim, Christian; she wondered now whether he had featured in Alice's nightmares too.

Alice had drawn the Pilgrim down in a corner of the page—at least, that was what Anne thought at first, because what was most noticeable about the tiny figure was the burden it carried on its back, which protruded like a hiker's rucksack. Only, when she peered more closely, she saw that the figure was not attired in coat and breeches and tall hat, as the Pilgrim ought to have been. It was wearing a long dress, and had a plain white cap on its head. Then Anne knew that this was not the Pilgrim at all. Alice had drawn herself.

The spells were at the back of the book. Most involved medicines made with herbs, and some were simple. *Ane Charme for the Toothaik* would work if you offered the sufferer an infusion of *bee plante and penney royale*, while uttering the words, *Shake from thee thy harme, shake from thee they siknes, shake from thee thy toothaik, in name of Father, in name of Sonne, in name of Haly Ghaist.* Others were more complicated, demanding that their ingredients be gathered *on St. Johnnes Eve*, or *under ful mune*. Warts were to be cured by dabbing each one with a cloth dipped in pig's blood. The cloth was then to be left by the road, and the warts would be transferred to the hands of the first person who picked it up. But all the charms, even this rather unfair one, were accompanied by some version of the words, *In the name of the Father, and of the Son, and of the Holy Spirit.* Anne found it hard to understand why the Church should have objected to good deeds which so carefully gave God the credit.

These were, of course, the words engraved on the silver bands of the charm-stone. But making this connection in no way prepared Anne for the surprise which was in store for her. The last of the spells was on a page by itself, and as she read it, she could feel her eyelids stretching with astonishment, and a stiffness afflicting her back. *To cure ills by the White Glasse from Uplawmuir, gift to mee, Alyce Jardyne, by my mother and my mother's mother. Taik water from a well . . .* There was not the slightest doubt in Anne's mind that she was reading about the stone which her own mother had found in the Grey Mound of Deer, and which now lay, attached to a tawdry twentieth-century chain, on the table beside her bed.

There had not been the slightest doubt in Alice's mind, either, that the White Glasse bequeathed by her mother was a stone of power, which could perform miracles of healing. She had detailed the charms which must be passed through the well-water—*ane silver pees, ane infants haire, ane stick of the birch*—before the stone was dipped three times, and the incantation spoken. *I sall dip thee in this water, thou cleer gem of power, in the name of the Apostles twelve, in the name of the high Trinitie, a blessing on the water, a healing to this hurt, and to this suffering creature.*

And, as if this were not astounding enough, underneath these words was a carefully inscribed list, which made Anne very thoughtful.

*Anthony Johnstoun, made haill of the falling siknes
Ane tinkers boy, of the fever
Patrick Moffitt, of sores to his face
ten kine, of the murrain
Mungo Dick, stabler to Mr Maxtoun, of the glanders
Marian Cunninghame, of the palsy*

Palsy. That was what was the matter with Polly. Nowadays it was called paralysis. Infantile paralysis was another name for polio. Although it didn't just attack infants, Anne knew that nearly all its victims were young people.

As she put out the light, and pulled the bedclothes up round her ears, Anne could not help wondering whether the charm-stone, which she was sure had once opened a window for her into the past of its owner, still retained some of its ancient, healing power. She was so busy thinking about this that she quite forgot another puzzling question. How had such a precious and prized possession been lost in the Grey Mound of Deer?

Anne had not expected to sleep well, but she did, waking only twice, puzzled by the unaccustomed feel of a strange bed in the darkness. But then she remembered where she was, turned over, and slept again. At half-past eight Mrs Armitage arrived with a breakfast tray, and opened the curtains, letting in a flood of clear light from a sunlit sky.

'The rain's away,' she told Anne. 'You'll have a nice run home.'

As Anne ate her scrambled egg, she wondered whether she would see Polly again before she left, or whether Major Jardine might come to see her off. That would be a pity, as she was dying to show Polly the page in Alice's book which told of the charm-stone. When Mrs Armitage came back to fetch the tray, however, she said, 'Mrs Jardine would like to see you before you go, Anne. Her room is next door to yours, on the left.'

'Oh, great,' said Anne. 'I'd like to see her, too. She's nice, isn't she?'

The housekeeper smiled at her.

'I think so,' she replied. 'She has a great deal to put up with, and she gives very little trouble to anyone.'

'She says she's bad-tempered,' Anne told her.

'Yes, I'm sure she does. She has a habit of painting herself as black as possible,' said Mrs Armitage calmly.

'You mean it isn't true?'

'Of course it isn't true. She's a brave girl, a soldier's daughter and a soldier's wife, and she doesn't complain.' Mrs Armitage frowned, and went on, 'Sometimes I think it would be better for her if she could cry, and make a fuss—it would give her some relief. It's such an unnatural life for a young woman. At her age, she should be running around, bringing up children and having some fun, not sitting in this empty house, thinking about the baby she lost, and how different it might have been. Barely twenty, she was, and they'd been married for less than a year. It's small wonder she gets irritable about little things, like there being withered flowers in a vase, or the curtains not hanging straight. But bad-tempered is far too strong a way of putting it.'

'I didn't believe she was,' Anne said.

Mrs Armitage picked up the tray, then she looked appealingly at Anne, and said, 'She loved having you here yesterday. It was a treat to pass the door and hear her laughing. Will you come and visit her again?'

'If she wants me to,' said Anne.

When she got up, she had another deep, scented bath, while the going was good, then she got dressed, picked up her blazer and Alice Jardyne's book, and made her way to Polly's room.

This was another large space with a sea-filled window, pale grey walls, and most of the furniture pushed back against them. But there were a few chairs, and as she went in Anne saw, propped against one of them, Polly's callipers and crutches. The sight of these objects caused an uncomfortable feeling in her chest, bringing home to her, as nothing had yesterday, the utterly exhausting, daily misery of being Polly Jardine.

Not that she was looking at all miserable at the moment. From the large white bed where she was sitting up with the Sunday newspapers spread out around her, she greeted Anne cheerfully. 'Good-morning. Have you slept well?'

Anne said that she had. 'And I've had two baths, to make up for the inch of tepid water and carbolic soap that I get at home.'

'I'm glad we're able to please you,' said Polly, amused. She lay back on her pillows, patted the counterpane beside her, and added, 'Come and sit down for a minute, and tell me—did you read Alice's book?'

'Yes,' Anne told her. 'I did. *And* I've got something to show you.'

She opened the book in front of Polly, and while she was looking at it, pulled the charm-stone from inside her blouse. She sat swinging it to and fro on the end of its chain, watching, and waiting for Polly to make the connection. When she did, her reaction was as wide-eyed as Anne could have hoped for.

'Well, I never! Fancy that! How very exciting! It never occurred to me when you showed me the stone yesterday — although to be fair to myself, until your letter arrived I hadn't looked at the book for ages. Of course it must be the same one, mustn't it, Anne? But how in the world did it get inside the Grey Mound?'

Anne had not got around to considering this question yet, and she waved it aside, drawing Polly's attention instead to the names of those Alice Jardyne claimed to have cured with the charm-stone.

'It looks impressive, doesn't it?' she urged. 'I mean, she was obviously a very religious person, and she wouldn't have told lies.'

But the response was gently crushing.

'No, she wouldn't. But she wasn't a very scientific person either, and one must ask how many of these people would have got better anyway.' Whereupon Polly firmly changed the subject. 'Anne, will you come and see me again?'

'Yes, please. I'd love to. When?'

Polly smiled wryly.

'I'm usually at home,' she said. 'Don't come on Thursday. That's the day the physiotherapist comes, and I'm always tired and cross in the afternoon. And not Sunday, Anne, because I spend the day with Johnny.'

Which explained her radiance this morning, Anne thought.

'What are you going to do today?' she asked.

'I don't know. Johnny has gone to see if it's warm enough for me to go out. If it is, we're going to take a picnic up to Moniaive. When will you come again, Anne?'

Anne said that Friday would be best, after school, when she had no homework to do for the next day. Then she thanked Polly, and said goodbye, and went out into the rain-washed morning.

13

Couples

A few days later, summer came in earnest. It was now the first week in June, the Burnet rose was in bud, and leaves had turned a more determined green. Under the sun, Marymount gym tunics were shed in favour of grey and white cotton frocks, and swotting for exams was combined with sunbathing on scorching travel-rugs on the lawn. The Seniors ordered the Juniors off the tennis-courts, and through open windows floated the voices of the School Choir, practising for Speech Day.

It was a lover and his lass,
With a hey, and a ho, and a hey nonino,
That o'er the green cornfield did pass
In the spring time, the only pretty ring time . . .

Jenny, resplendent in her Senior Prefect's uniform, was enjoying her last days of great importance; she was realist enough to know that she would never be so eminent again, unless she became Matron of a hospital. Anne, whose lack of team spirit had been mentioned sourly on her last report, would never be a Marymount prefect. The only thing she wanted was what a well-organized girls' school could never give her, peace to be herself.

Meanwhile, away from school, the life of Deer was moving inexorably towards its dissolution. Mr Russell had been appointed to a new parish in Aberdeenshire. The cottagers were taken by bus to see the houses which had been built for them up behind the dam, and came back vastly pleased. Miss Groom heard that she was to be given the school at Kirkton in the next valley, and told Mrs Farrar that she was delighted, having feared a forced move to a town school. Anne observed with interest that none of the Deer people seemed at all distressed by the drowning of the Valley, where their forebears had lived for centuries. They were all cheerfully looking forward to a new life elsewhere. It was the Farrars, strangers and outsiders, who cared most. Dr and Mrs Farrar could excavate the Grey Mound, and save its treasures, but the Grey Mound itself would be lost for ever, while Anne was haunted in her imagination by the unfolding loveliness of flowers and trees that, after this one summer, would never see the light again.

She tried to tell Polly something of this, when she was having tea with her on Friday, after school. Polly replied that she understood exactly how Anne felt.

'I've never wanted to go back to Deer,' she confessed. 'It would be too painful. We meant to live at the Owls' House, and we had all sorts of plans for what we would do with it. It's such a lovely house, Anne, don't you think? Johnny says isn't it a mercy, now, that we didn't spend a fortune on it, which is probably true, but all these seven years I've felt it would break my heart to see the pink gillyflowers in the courtyard, and hear the bees humming in the honeysuckle outside the back door. Yet I've liked to think they were still there, even if I couldn't see them, and it's horrible to know they're going to be obliterated in such a way.'

Which was when Anne said, almost without thinking, 'Except that they needn't be. We could rescue them and bring them here.'

There was silence for a moment, while Polly looked at her with the grey eyes which could smile, and look amused, but which had become blind to hope long ago.

'Could we?' she said uncertainly. 'How could we?'

They were sitting in a little paved courtyard at the back of the house, looking out on uninteresting lawns, and flower-beds peppered with dusty, unloved shrubs.

'Easily,' replied Anne emphatically, as the idea sparked by her own casual remark suddenly caught fire. 'I could dig the flowers up, and wrap them in wet newspaper, and ask

Daddy or Ben to bring them over in the car. Then we could plant them out here. You've got plenty of room, haven't you? Oh, Polly, do say yes. It would be such fun.'

'Fun,' repeated Polly, trying the word out. 'But Anne, you don't understand. I can't do anything.'

'You can do the planning,' Anne told her firmly, 'and I'll do the digging, and the planting. You could put some of the plants into pots, and I expect you could do a bit of raking and watering, couldn't you?'

'Perhaps. I would try,' said Polly, adding longingly, 'Oh, Anne, do you really suppose we could? I don't know the first thing about gardening.'

'Neither do I,' confessed Anne. 'We'll have to learn together.'

Anne explained to Polly that she had exams all the next week, and said she would come again when they were over. She advised Polly to get rid of her shrubs, and have some manure dug into her flower-beds. 'That much I do know,' she said, laughing. Polly promised to attend to this. Then Anne caught the rattling, wooden-seated, left-over-from-wartime bus, which passed Maryfield House at twenty to six. It lumbered all round the Bay, shuddered its way through two valleys, and arrived at Deer Post Office at half-past seven.

'I thought I'd never get here,' she remarked to her mother as she came, stiff and weary, into the kitchen, and lowered herself on to a chair.

'I'd have come to fetch you, if I'd known it would take so long,' said Mrs Farrar, who was heating up the inevitable baked beans on the Calor-gas stove, with *Archaeology Now* dangerously propped up beside the grill-pan.

'Would you?' asked Anne, incredulously. Mrs Farrar was famous for always being far too busy to offer this normal, motherly kind of service. At least it had made her daughters independent.

'Oh, I'd have come for Mrs Jardine's sake,' she now replied. 'She might have liked to have you stay a little longer.'

'Have you met her, Mother?' enquired Anne curiously. She realized that her mother had known, the day she had been so cock-a-hoop over her ritual fire-pit, that Polly had had polio; knowing Mrs Farrar, she was not at all surprised that she had failed to mention it.

'Once,' said Mrs Farrar, lifting her beans off the stove. 'I had to go over to see the young man about something—I forget what—and they asked me to have coffee with them. A brave, desperate girl, I thought. Such restless hands. I'd never cared for the Major, until then, but I must say he was very gentle with her.'

'She thinks he's marvellous,' Anne told her.

'I got the impression that feeling was mutual,' said her mother.

The next day, however, Mrs Farrar proved less sympathetic to another loving couple.

On Saturday morning, what Dr Farrar referred to as an Atmosphere descended on the Owls' House. The cause was simple. Meeting her in the yard before breakfast, Ben had invited Jenny to go with him in the evening to the cinema in Dumfries, to see Charlie Chaplin and Claire Bloom in *Limelight*. Jenny's joy was full-throated, but before she even had time to get her best frock out of the wardrobe, Mrs Farrar had destroyed her happiness with three words, 'You're not going.' There was more, along the lines that sixteen was far too young to be going out alone with a man, and that those who frequented the back row of the stalls in a provincial cinema were rarely there to see the film. Jenny pleaded, but to no avail. She was told that she might go if Ben invited Anne to accompany them. Anne said, thanks, but she would rather die, and Jenny said, so would she.

As usual, when there was an Atmosphere, the family scattered. Mrs Farrar stalked loftily into the study, and Dr Farrar found that he had to be very busy upstairs in the skeleton's room, analysing some cremated bones. It was Anne who was inconvenienced most. If she wanted to lie low in her bedroom, Jenny was there, sniffing. If she wanted to go into the bathroom, Jenny was sniffing in there. The day wore on heavily, with burnt sausages for lunch. But then, in the middle of the afternoon, the Atmosphere was unexpectedly dissolved by Dr Farrar's taking Jenny's side.

'In six months' time,' he pointed out to his wife, 'she'll have left home, and we'll have to trust her. Don't you think we might as well have a trial run of trusting her now?'

Anne was only an onlooker here, but she knew what trusting meant. Old-fashioned though she might be in some respects, Mrs Farrar had not shirked telling her daughters what were then called the Facts of Life. Anne, like most girls, knew that her mother's high moral principle about the need for sex to be within a loving marriage, for the children's sake, was offset by a less noble-minded horror of becoming an illegitimate grand-mother. But now, she thought that Mrs Farrar was simply being absurd. Did she really imagine that Ben would be swept away by uncontrollable passion, and Jenny fated to become an unmarried mother between the bus-stop at Deer and the flicks in Dumfries? Would Jenny really be any more trustworthy in August, when she would be seventeen? If Polly Jardine had been engaged to Johnny in the last year of the war, Anne reflected, she could only have been a few months older than Jenny was now. What would Mrs Farrar say about that?

Perhaps Mrs Farrar did secretly realize that she was being unreasonable, because she gave in, contenting herself with giving Ben strict orders that Jenny was to be home by ten o'clock. Ben said, 'Oh, yes, of course, Dr Farrar,' with such a solemnly virtuous air that Anne had to run out and giggle in the scullery.

So Jenny's misery was turned to radiance, and at half-past five Anne watched her running down the lane to meet Ben in her pink and navy polka-dot frock, curled, lipsticked and handbagged, her strong legs twinkling in high-heeled shoes and nylon stockings with their seams spiralling her calves. For the first time ever, Anne experienced an attack of affection for Jenny, of the kind she sometimes felt for her parents. She thought she might even get quite fond of Jenny, once she didn't have to share a bed with her, and see her every day.

That evening, herself as yet untouched by love, Anne went out of doors with a notebook, and made a list of all the flowers in the neglected garden which might be pried clear of the weeds, and transplanted into the forlorn flower-beds of Maryfield House. Besides the pink and white carnations which Polly called gillyflowers, there were marguerites and lily-of-the-valley, lavender, thrift and maiden-pinks, columbine and Sweet William, huge red poppies and Canterbury bells. Then there were the bulbs of snowdrops, daffodils and creamy crocuses, and leafy clumps of delphinium and Michaelmas daisy, their flowering yet to come. She copied the list on to a sheet of writing paper and posted it to Polly, with a note suggesting that she might make a start on a garden plan.

On the way back from the postbox, she fell to thinking about Alice Jardyne, and wondering, as she had at the Witch's Cottage, how many of these flowers had seeded themselves down the years from ones which she had planted. For Polly had said that Alice loved her garden, in the good days, before Christian Grahame cast a dark shadow over her life.

14

Pageant

During the busy summer days that followed, the memory of Alice Jardyne, the gentle little hunchback fated to suffer in the darkest, most cruel years of her country's history, haunted Anne's mind, to the point of obsession. There were many things to be done, exams to be tackled, the first planting of Polly's garden to be arranged, rehearsals for the Pageant of Deer to be attended. But always, whatever she was doing, Alice Jardyne was there in Anne's imagination, dark-skinned and brown-eyed, wearing a plaid shawl over her neat brown dress. Sometimes Anne visualized her in the kitchen of the Owls' House, as nimble about her tasks with one hand as anyone else with two; sometimes she met her in the wood in a wide-brimmed straw hat, with a basket of herbs on her good arm. If she went up on Cairnshee for a Sunday ramble with Jenny, she thought she glimpsed her in the garden of the Witch's Cottage, where pale pink summer roses scrambled over the walls, and Queen of the Meadow pushed up among the fading leaves of daffodils.

At Polly's house, in breaks between stints of gardening, Anne pored over Alice's manuscript book, admiring her drawings of plants and flowers, reading her recipes and pondering her spells. At home, she reread *The Pilgrim's Progress*, and at school where, after the exams were over, the girls were encouraged to spend the last weeks of term exploring topics which interested them, she chose the time when Alice Jardyne had lived. Studying in the library *Domestic Life in Scotland 1650–1750*, and *Religion and Folk-Beliefs of the Scottish Borders*, she created a world to contain Alice which was in a sense imaginary, and in a sense real. All that remained now, she thought, to complete the story of that short, tragic life was to find out what had happened after Alice was dragged off to imprisonment in Kirkcudbright Tolbooth. Anne knew all too well that alternative endings were few, and could only hope against hope that the blotting out, when it came, was mercifully quick.

Also unsolved, of course, was the intriguing puzzle of how the charm-stone, the 'White Glasse from Uplawmuir', had found its way into the Grey Mound of Deer. Anne had discussed this with Polly, and they were agreed that the mystery was unfathomable. It might, as Polly said, have passed from Alice's hands into those of other members of the family, so that its getting into the Mound might have no connection with Alice's story at all. No line of inquiry seemed open, and if, as Anne believed and Polly did not, the stone itself had the power to reveal things, it was not co-operating at the moment. This difference of opinion Anne and Polly did not discuss; there seemed no point, since neither was likely to dent the conviction of the other. To Polly, the notion that a stone might have magical powers was too absurd to contemplate, while Anne, stubbornly convinced of her own experience, went on believing. And when, from time to time, she read the names of those whom Alice Jardyne had cured with the White Glasse, she dreamed of a day when she would make Polly Jardine repent her lack of faith.

Polly did not mention Alice Jardyne often, although Anne suspected that she too frequently had her in mind. When the exams were over, and there was little homework to be done, Anne began to spend most of her spare time at Maryfield House. Although there were thirteen years between them in age, she and Polly found friendship easy. To Polly, Anne was like a much younger sister who had the blessed gift of unobtrusive helpfulness; she quietly did the things which Polly couldn't do, and left her to do the things she could. Polly was grateful for Anne's companionship, which filled a void of loneliness in her life; her family and friends were far away in the south of England, while

Johnny, with three farms, forty miles apart, to look after could not spend much time with her.

Anne's feelings for Polly were more complicated. On one level, since she had failed to find an intimate friend at Marymount, Polly's friendship meant as much to her as hers did to Polly. Polly was the elder sister who liked her, and didn't boss her about; Anne admired her looks, her style and her taste as much as she deprecated Jenny's. But, being Anne, she could not resist investing Polly with a romantic aura which she would certainly have disclaimed: the girl who had had polio in 1947, and was confined to a stone and concrete country house in 1954, would have found it difficult to recognize herself as a legendary princess in a tower, under a strong, but perhaps reversible, enchantment. She would also have been outraged by the comparison, and would have told Anne roundly how silly and dangerous it was to live in a world where no distinction was made between reality and make-believe.

In the real world, however, the scheme of creating a garden at Maryfield with the doomed flowers of Deer was proving a great success. The plants which Anne dug up at Owls' House were willingly transported to Dunchree by Mrs Farrar, who was usually shy and rather formal with strangers, but treated Polly with the casual gentleness she showed to her own daughters. When Anne wasn't there to help with the planting, Polly spent her time surrounded by piles of books on gardening, bought for her in Glasgow by a relieved and delighted Johnny. Sitting at the kitchen table, she planted seeds in boxes and geraniums in terracotta pots, soiling her hands and getting earth behind her beautifully-kept fingernails. One day, Polly would be an expert gardener, and an authority on gardening for disabled people, but now she was just a girl engrossed in a new hobby. And she was happier than she had been for seven years.

The flowers from the Owls' House took hold in the Maryfield soil and flourished. Ben brought cuttings of the honeysuckle and planted them where they would grow up around the front door. Miss Groom sent a root of her

Christmas rose, which was planted outside Polly's bedroom window.

'I remember that girl,' she said gruffly to Anne, when she heard what was going on. 'I liked her. Ask her if she wants a cutting of my Japanese quince as well.'

Meanwhile, preparations for the Pageant of Deer went on apace. Great crates of clothes arrived at the Church Hall from a theatrical costumier's in Manchester; doublets, hoods, hose, farthingales and wigs were tried on amid howls of laughter, while Mrs Russell scuttled to and fro, red and perspiring, trying in vain to keep order.

'*Please*, people, a little less noise would be helpful. Oh, *please*!'

'If that woman doesn't lay an egg before the twenty-third, it will be miraculous,' remarked Helen Elliot, a fellow witch, to Anne, as they tried on their long wigs and brown tatters. The witches were becoming quite friendly, just as the time approached when they would never see one another again. Anne laughed, and agreed with this, but she was looking at her costume with another access of the unease which this enterprise had aroused in her from the beginning, and which she still did not entirely understand. Not until the clothes had been packed away again in their boxes did she feel better.

On Thursday the twenty-first, the stage, stands and marquees were erected in the School Field by young men under the supervision of Mr Maxton, a descendant, Anne supposed, of the farmer whose stableman had been cured of glanders by the White Glasse of Uplawmuir. In the evening, wooden crates of lemonade bottles were delivered, and crockery was carried over from the Church Hall, along with card-tables, folding chairs and tea-urns. The ladies of the Women's Guild moved in purposefully, and it was evident that, however appalling the dramatic performance, the last teas ever served at Deer would be of the traditional high standard.

On Friday, black clouds marched triumphantly over the blue sky, and the evening Dress Rehearsal was a chaotic affair, marred by spots of rain, rising wind, and almost everybody forgetting their lines. Mrs Russell complained of a headache, clutched her brow, and cried, 'Never again,' while Miss Groom grinned sardonically in a deck-chair.

Up on the summit of Cairnshee, above the Witch's Cottage, a vast stack of wood, heather and broom had been prepared by the 1st Deer Troop of the Boy Scouts. The Midsummer Bonfire was to be lit at ten o'clock on Saturday night, and the children, at least, were looking forward to it far more than to the Pageant. Mr Russell, who was in charge of the Bonfire, had been investigating old customs, and instructing the Scouts in a 'Leaping Dance', which he said dated back to Celtic times. Mrs Farrar said it dated back to the last week in May, when Mr Russell invented it, and they had a tiff outside the Post Office. Ben, who happened to be buying stamps at the time, afterwards gave a gleeful account of this exchange to Jenny and Anne.

'She plastered him all over the pavement,' he said with relish. 'That'll teach him to accuse her of middle-class affectation. Good old Sadie—I was proud of her.'

'I wonder what she'll wear on Speech Day,' said Jenny gloomily.

Despite her dislike of her role, and her inability to rid her mind of Alice Jardyne, Anne managed to enjoy the Dress Rehearsal. Although she never chose to go around in a gang, she liked company occasionally, and it was fun to sit on the grass with the rest of the cast, watching things go wrong, being teased by the boys of the Pipe Band, and eating the supper of fish and chips which a young Maxton shot off in his Austin A30 to fetch from the chip shop at Kirkton. She thought Jenny was excruciating as Mary, Queen of Scots—*'Prithee weep not, my good Abbot. Shall not tomorrow see the end of all our woes?'*—and that the little boys from the village school looked sweet, slapping their thighs and skipping, with scarlet faces and expressions which would have soured milk. There was a long delay when the microphone went dead, and it was nearly ten o'clock before, in a cloud of midges, the witches went on stage, to reel and jig to the wild music of Henry

Groom's bagpipes. Anne's song sounded wild too, the voice not her own, as loudspeakers threw it around the darkening field. At half-past ten, she and Jenny walked home together.

It was when she woke up, in the fragile half-dark of the summer night, and saw the witch's tattered brown dress and black wig hanging on the back of the door, that misgivings again assailed Anne, more powerfully than ever before. And with the misgivings came, for the first time, a full understanding of them. She had always known that her feeling went far deeper than Miss Groom's decent distaste for making entertainment out of suffering, but for weeks she had been managing to keep distress at bay by assuring herself that the Witches' Dance was a nonsense which had nothing to do with Alice Jardyne. She had been comforted, to some extent, by Polly's words, 'Whatever it was like, it wasn't like that,' but, deep down, she had known that she was doing something of which she was ashamed.

Because—of course—what she felt did have to do with Alice Jardyne, who had leapt out of history to become someone whom Anne knew. It was the first sight of that black wig, when the costumes had arrived from Manchester, which had started the trickle of remorse which now became a flood. For as she lay looking at the wig, and the deliberately slashed garment which she must wear tomorrow, she could not help remembering Alice Jardyne, whom she had seen running through Hoolets' Wood with death in her eyes, black hair flying, and wearing just such a dress. Little Alice, who had bought three yards of gingham for a gown, who loved animals and flowers, who had cared for the sick, and had come, in the end, to look like the witch her neighbours said she was. It would be Alice Jardyne, not any other nameless witch, whom Anne would travesty by wearing these clothes tomorrow, giving the lie to Alice's innocence by dancing to the Devil's pipes. And lying at Jenny's side, she wept stiffly and silently, because in her own eyes she was betraying a friend.

She slept only fitfully after that, drifting through dreams

in which she was Alice Jardyne, fleeing from unseen foes, and saw Johnny and Polly, walking hand in hand beside a great lake of black water, under an icy moon.

Mrs Russell's last words on Friday had been, 'Now, everybody, remember to say your prayers for a nice day tomorrow!' Anne had not felt it necessary to obey this instruction, but perhaps others had, since by getting-up time the wind had blown itself away, the clouds had withdrawn, and the sun was shining sharply in the eastern sky. So there was no hope of a cancellation. During the morning, Anne wondered whether she might feign illness severe enough to result in her being sent to bed, but decided not. Mrs Farrar always knew when you were ill, but was also pretty quick at detecting when you were not. Besides, she knew that she could only be true to the dead Alice Jardyne, so late in the day, by letting down the living Miss Groom. Eight dancers were needed for the reel, and she was the only one who could sing. However much she hated it, she must go through with it now, and hope that Alice would have forgiven her—she could not say, 'would have understood', for she knew that the present would be as incomprehensible to Alice Jardyne as much of the past was to Anne.

By the time she arrived at the field at half-past one, already in her witch's dress, and carrying her plaid and wig in a brown paper bag, the grass was pale and shimmering under a relentless midsummer sun. As she waited in the queue in the marquee to have some grease-paint slapped on her face, the smell, a mixture of enclosed grass, grubby costumes and perspiration, made her feel sick. Her stomach turned, and she began to feel oddly detached from what was going on around her. When she had put on her dancing pumps, she took her plaid and wig to the chairs where the performers were to sit while waiting to go on, and was glad when Mr Maxton came, and told them to move to the other end of the field, where there were some trees. But the shade made only a little difference. Beyond the tree-shadow the glare was almost unbearable, and she kept having to take off her glasses to wipe away the perspiration running down the sides of her nose. She knew from the amount of brown grease-paint on her handkerchief that her face must now be a very odd sight, but she was too tired to care.

Afterwards, Anne could remember that afternoon only as a series of images, like snapshots with no obvious sequence. Her parents, dressed unexceptionally, she in cream linen and he in a grey suit, yet still looking like two rare birds that had strayed into a hen-run. Jenny, in pink brocade with a white ruff and velvet cap, having the time of her life in spite of the heat. Henry Groom, sitting along from her with his horned Devil's head-dress on his knee—had Alice Jardyne been burned to death because people said she had sold her soul to a Devil no more real than that absurdity of papier mâché and poster paint? Then there was Jenny's little page, spilling ice-cream on his breeches, and Miss Groom, furtively smoking a cigarette behind the hedge. And in all the heat, Anne could feel the charm-stone of Alice Jardyne, lying like a lump of ice against her chest.

At four o'clock, she put on the wig and plaid, and, dressed like an insult to the memory of someone she loved, she danced, leaping and kicking her heels to the horrible music of this implacably foreign land. And she sang, because she must, and was thankful that she need never hear that song again. There was applause from the audience, who sat shaded in the stand or broiling on the benches, and a last snapshot; Mrs Russell, like a smiling lobster with a bouquet of red roses, waving and saying how jolly it had all been.

Then Anne went home with her parents, and went to bed, and slept until seven o'clock.

'You don't have to go to the Bonfire if you don't want to, my love,' said Mrs Farrar to Anne, as they ate Jenny's spam salad in the cool of the evening. 'If you ask me, you've had enough for today.' Anne was the less sturdy of her daughters, and Mrs Farrar was uneasily aware, sometimes, of the toll her imagining took of the strength

93

she had. She had no idea what had been troubling Anne today, but she knew that she had been troubled.

However Anne said she would like to go. She thought that the worst must surely be over, with the ending of the dance.

15

Witch!

The Farrars left the Owls' House just after nine, joining the happy, relaxed procession of villagers climbing the path which wound upwards through Hoolets' Wood, then over heather-clad moorland to the top of Cairnshee. The swelter of the afternoon had cooled to a pleasant, airy evening, the sky was silver-pale behind the sharp blue edge of the hill, the harebells luminous in the translucent northern night. Dr and Mrs Farrar, gently warned by Jenny that no one really wanted to hear learned talk about the Celtic sun-rituals, chatted quite normally with their neighbours about the events of the day, Ben and Jenny loitered behind to hold hands, and Anne walked alone. Although she felt recovered in her body after her sleep, the heat had left her mind strangely empty and fatigued. She felt that filling it with thought would be too great an effort, and she did not want to talk to anyone.

As they rounded the shoulder of the hill, the dark mass of the Bonfire, eight feet tall and seven across, reared up against the sky. Standing back from it were the figures of those climbers who had already made it to the top. When they reached the ruin of the Witch's Cottage, its garden a tangle of glowing colours and mysterious night-shapes, sounds began to float down to them, children's high voices, a piano-accordion, the pulpit-boom of Mr Russell, directing things. Here Anne stopped, leaning against the tumbledown wall, and waited for her parents to catch her up. Then she went on with them to the summit.

The top of Cairnshee, highest of the Valley hills, was a platform of crumbly earth and patchy, sheep-cropped grass. There were perhaps a hundred and fifty people, by the time the stragglers had arrived, all grouped around the dark, sinister pile. Mr Russell, greatly daring in the presence of Mrs Farrar, gave a little talk about the tradition of bonfire-lighting on Cairnshee through the ages, and how it had only been discontinued during the First World War. Various heathen customs and superstitions had been carried on into Christian times, he said, such as the May Day custom of sprinkling water on cattle to keep them healthy, and dancing to drive away the threat of witchcraft at Midsummer. He then invited his wife to perform the lighting ceremony.

There was a pause, while a torch dipped in pitch and kerosene was lit, then Anne had a glimpse of Mrs Russell, like the Statue of Liberty, holding it aloft before thrusting it into the side of the stack. There was an expectant silence as smoke crept through the crevices in the wood, a flicker within, a rosy glow. Then suddenly through the roof of the pile, flames put out their tongues and tasted the air. Up they sprang, russet-brown, scarlet and gold. Adults clapped, children screamed and whooped, and the man with the piano-accordion started to play. Scouts, naked to the waist and smeared with soot, moved to their positions for Mr Russell's 'Leaping Dance'. Mrs Farrar was unable any longer to resist sharing her opinion with those near enough to hear. Her clear English voice rang out confidently.

'The claim that evidence exists for such a survival from the Celtic period is frankly inadmissible, and . . .'

'Just wait till I get her home,' hissed Jenny, between her teeth.

Anne did not hear a word her mother was saying. She had not heard much of Mr Russell's discourse either, although the words, 'dancing to drive away the threat of witchcraft at Midsummer', had sounded familiarly in the airy chamber of her head, like an echo of something she had heard before. The noise of stamping feet and voices raised excitedly above the roar of the flames seemed vaguely familiar too, but she could only concentrate through her eyes.

Frightened and fascinated, Anne stared into the

furnace-heart of the great fire, cruelly beautiful, outshining the setting sun. Flames sprang eagerly upwards, and explosions in the wood sent sprays of sparks towards a blood-coloured sky. Then someone began to set off fireworks. Squibs cracked, and rockets zipped into the air, bursting in rival spark-showers, pink, purple and green. A small child on Anne's left began to scream, and somewhere to her right a piper began to tune up his bagpipes. That was when she knew she could stand no more of this. Quietly, she slipped back to the edge of the crowd, and began to hurry down the track into the lee of the hill. She would seek shelter in the Witch's Cottage, and when all this barbarous merry-making was over, she would find her mother, and go home.

It was relief beyond measure to make her way up the rose-scented ghost-path through Alice's garden, and step over the doorless threshold into the unroofed interior of the cottage. It was one small room, turf-carpeted, its only furniture lumps of fallen masonry and a pile of rubbish left by untidy picnickers. High above her, the sky was a reflected flutter of light, the noise of music and excited voices still audible, but mercifully distanced. Exhausted as she had never been in her life before, Anne sat down on the ground, under the vacant window, with her back to the wall, and her knees drawn up to her chest. To shut out the disturbing flicker in the sky, she put her forehead on her knees, and closed her eyes. Instinctively, her fingers found their way under her jersey, and curled themselves around the cold charm-stone. She sat like that in the darkness for a long time, thinking of nothing, until an identity not her own came to occupy the empty space that her mind had become. Then she had the most singular experience of her whole life.

She thought she had been sitting here on the floor all day, with her head well down below the level of the sill. The summer heat had never touched her, and now she was cold, so cold she thought she could never be warm again. Yet she dared not rise, and kindle a fire on her little hearth, because smoke and light would remind her enemies of her presence. They had been watching her for a long time now, half-afraid of her still, but this was a night of special danger, Midsummer Eve, the Night of St. John, when garlands of potent herbs were burned in the Midsummer Fire, to drive away witches and evil spirits. She had made the garlands herself, many times, never thinking that one terrible day she would herself be the outcast, the shunned and evil one. God alone knew what ideas the wild fire above would put into their excited, fuddled heads; she must keep very quiet, and pray that in their drunkenness they would forget, and pass her by.

They had been preparing the ground for the Bonfire for days, up the track there on the bare crest of Cairnshee, and she had watched them, made furtive against her nature, from behind the shutter of the cottage's one window. After the men had dug the pit where the fire would be contained, they had gone away, and the children had come, bearing armfuls of twigs, furze, broom, whatever would burn brightly, and thrown them into the pit. They had made many journeys, and she had heard their voices, shrill with excitement, as they came and went on the path that ran along the margin of her herb garden. But when she went and stood openly at the door, they fell silent, nudging each other, and glanced away, so that she knew they had been warned not to speak to her. This was the point where hurt could still pierce the terror which, once again, was driving out all other sensations, for three of these were the young ones of the widow Cunninghame, whose palsy she had cured. But the widow Cunninghame was a crony now of her own good-sister, Christian Jardyne, and favours were soon forgotten.

As for the others, poor monkeys, they knew no better. But it hurt, because she liked children, though she had borne none of her own, and some of these she had thought of as friends. Before Christian had driven her away from Hoolets' Farm, and the whispering began, they had come with her on her plant-gathering expeditions along the lanes, helping her to carry her basket, and never seeming to mind her warped shoulder, and her useless, claw-like hand. She had felt at ease in their company. Not any more, though.

Yesterday, greatly daring, for she feared the dogs and the stones, she had done something she felt she must, knowing that the end was in sight, whatever the end might be. Taking her leather-bound book, her Bible, and her precious copy of Mr Bunyan's *Pilgrim* from the press, she had wrapped them in her plaid, and carried them down to her brother at Hoolets'. Her good-sister had not wanted to let her past the gate, where her own bonny rowan-tree was now meant to guard the threshold of her home against her. For witches could not pass a rowan-tree. She would have liked to see her father, to beg his forgiveness for the sorrow she had brought upon him, for the sin she had never committed. But when she saw that sneering, flinty face in the window, she had known that that wish was doomed never to be fulfilled. Rob had taken the books kindly enough, and had listened to her request that they should be given to her sister Jennet, who had a daughter who might inherit the healing gift. She had seen the trouble in his brown eyes, and although she knew now that he would never make a move to save her, she took what comfort she could from his quiet, 'God go with thee.' Though where God was in such a terrible world was more than she could understand.

When she got back, having come a long way round to avoid Deer street, the fire had gone out. Feeling no hunger, yet aware that her body needed food, she had eaten some oatcake and drunk some water from the spring outside her door. Then she had said her evening prayer to the God who had forsaken her, laid aside her gown, and crawled into her sleeping-place, pulling the plaid over her tiny, crooked body.

All praise to thee, my God, this night
For all the blessings of the light,
Keep me, O keep me, King of Kings,
Beneath thine own almighty wings.

He had been there in the morning, a man, standing on

the path, staring at the cottage. No one she knew, just a man in black, staring, his shadow long and dark in the morning sun. After a while he turned and went away through the heather, but that was when fear had finally mastered her, and she sank down under the window in her brown shift, putting her head on her knees. She had sat there all day, except for the few minutes when she had crawled outside to pass water in the bracken, waiting. The sun beat down on the thatched roof, making the room hot and stuffy with the cloying scent of the herbs, hanging in bunches from the rafters. But she shivered, every nerve of her on edge, and the ache in her arm, which had never in all her life really gone away, intensified until she thought the pain would drive her mad.

The sun was far down when she heard them coming up the hill from the village, the dull thud of poorly-shod feet, the more precise tread of the animals, the pattering steps of the little ones. Raising her head cautiously, so that she could peep through the chink in the shutters, she glimpsed a line of dark, silent shadows, against a sky which hesitated between night and day. A hundred souls in all, perhaps, with two small horses, a score of thin sheep and a few pitiful cattle, the remnant of the herd they said she had slain. Later on, they would drive them through the powerful embers of the Midsummer Fire, to protect them from other poor women . . .

She huddled down again, and heard them go on up the track to the place of the cold, unlit fire. There was silence, for a long time. Then suddenly, just as she thought her head must crack under the strain, a great shout arose, signal that the fire had caught, and soared, killing the sky with its violent red and gold.

Then the stamping began, the wild mirth of the young men dancing, and she remembered, from the days before they cast her out, how they smeared themselves with the ashes until, with their blackened hands and faces, they seemed no longer of human kind. She listened, and watched through her fingers the red line drawn on the wall by the gap in the shutters, until the flames died down, and

100

the sky strengthened. Soon it would be dawn. But still, she knew, they continued to dance through the embers, driving the bleating, terrified beasts before them, and her body went rigid as the age-old words of their chant began to thud in her ears, 'Burn the witches! Burn, burn the witches!'

Even before she looked through the shutters, and saw them lurching down the slope, black-visaged demons in the light of the whirling torches, she was aware of her peril; even as her reason told her that flight was futile, some deeper urge ordered her to put up a fight. Springing up from the floor, she ran to her sleeping-place, grabbed her plaid, and tied it over her shoulders. She heard them trampling down the herb garden, but before the flames touched the thatch at the back of the house, she was out at the front. With the smell of smoke in her nostrils, and the crackle of dry straw in her ears, she resolved to run. Crippled in an arm she might be, but her feet were strong enough, and she would escape them if she could. Using her good hand to lift up her shift above her knees, she tucked her palsied arm into her bodice, and fled. With the thing that had surely condemned her pressed coldly to her breast, she flung away from her persecutors, down through the bracken, making for the thin oak wood which had once been a forest—as if any forest on earth could shelter her now.

16

The Grey Mound of Deer

Down, down, down. Down among the heather, in among the trees. Breathe deeply. Trip. Fall. Pick yourself up. Never mind the pain. It isn't broken. Never mind the blood. Make yourself run again.

Battered and terrified, running from an unseen horror which she dared not look round to see, Anne fought her way through the bracken and the bramble thicket, pressing the charm-stone to her with her left forearm, holding up her cotton dirndl-skirt, unnecessarily, in her right hand. She was scratched and bruised, but it scarcely seemed to matter; with the last coherent threads of her own, or someone else's mind, she knew only that she must get away. Run a little further, find somewhere to hide. Rest quietly through the day, then set out in darkness on a journey that must take her a thousand miles from this accursed place, begging her bread, but safe. Safe from *the pestilence that walketh in darkness, the destruction that wasteth at noonday.* Who said that? *I will say of my God, He is my refuge and my fortress; my God, in Him will I trust.* Not her words. Don't think. Don't cry out. Run.

But now she was clear of the trees, and that was dangerous. Down below her, in the thin dawn mist, she could see the dark bulk of Hoolets' Farm, solid in its hollow under the eaves of the wood. Empty, because all the farm folk, even the old father, were up on Cairnshee at the fire. But not safe, ever again. Where, then? For one moment she paused on the edge of the barley field, and looked out beyond the black roofs. Then she knew. That strange huddle of grey boulders across the road from the house, fronted by a half-ring of tall stones like broken teeth—was there not a slit in the roof, that a child, or a tiny adult could squeeze through, and drop down into the little earthy room below? Her tormentors were tall and well-grown, but she was the same size she had been at eleven—thinner, even, after all she had endured. Surely no one would think of looking for her there. Even to curl up and die in the dark would be better than the fate that awaited her if she were taken . . .

Summoning the last of her strength, she ran down the footpath that flanked Hoolets' Farm, flitted across the road, and made for the shelter of the Grey Mound. Confusedly, she heard voices behind her calling, 'Anne! Anne!' but that was not her name. With her bleeding right hand, she clawed her way up the side of the Mound, and lay along the top of it, feeling for the space. Thanks be to God, it was there. Only—in the last conscious moment of despair at the cruelty of life, she realized—her shape had changed, and she could not get through. As she slid, unprotesting, into darkness, she felt the chain around her neck snap. Something rolled away from her body, over the roof of the Mound. It did not matter what it was. Night covered her.

In the morning, when Anne woke up, she found her mother in the bed beside her, instead of Jenny. She moved when Anne moved, pushing herself up on her elbow, and said softly, 'Good-morning. How do you feel now?'

'I don't know,' Anne said. 'What time is it?'

'Ten to seven,' replied Mrs Farrar. 'I'm going to get up, but it's far too early for you to be waking. Close your eyes, and try to go to sleep again.'

Anne thought that this was a good idea, but although her eyes felt very heavy, sleep would not at first return to her. Instead, after her mother had slipped out of the bed and gone off to the bathroom, she lay on her back in the quiet morning, and slowly the events of the previous night began to come back into her mind.

The most recent incidents came first. She remembered

lying on her tummy on a high stone platform and hearing someone sobbing bitterly, long before she realized that it was herself. Then Jenny's voice saying, 'It's all right, Anne. Stop struggling, love. No one's going to hurt you. It's only Ben and me.' She had opened her eyes to find herself lying on grass, with their two faces above her. How absurd. When they were married, they would be Ben and Jen. She remembered that Ben had carried her into the house, and put her on the sofa in the study. Jenny had brought Dettol and Elastoplast, and had bathed her scratches before putting plasters on the cuts on her right hand. Then her mother had taken her upstairs, and put her into bed.

Recalling the events that lay behind these was more difficult. They had to do with Alice Jardyne, but so much that had happened recently had to do with Alice Jardyne. Something about a bonfire, and a kitchen, and a chase through woods. Anne thought she might remember better later, after she had had another little sleep.

The next time she woke, the sun was shining straight in at the little window, sending a dust-flecked shaft of brightness across the striped counterpane. She could hear the bell of Deer Kirk, sweetly monotonous, warning that it was time for morning service.

'It must be eleven o'clock,' she said out loud.

'Five to,' said Mrs Farrar, coming in with a breakfast tray. 'Can you sit up, and let me put this on your knee?'

Stiffly, Anne pulled herself up in the bed, and looked at the tray, opening her mouth to say, 'Thank you, Mother,' for the egg and the toast and marmalade. But when she saw what else was on the tray, words failed her.

'This seems to make a habit of getting into the Mound, doesn't it?' said Mrs Farrar lightly, picking up in her work-worn fingers the silver-banded crystal, still attached to its broken chain. 'I found it again this morning, in the same place.'

She put it down on the tray, and went away, and as Anne slowly ate her breakfast it all came back to her, where she had lost it, and how she had thought she was Alice Jardyne. All the horror of that terrible flight down

Cairnshee swept over her again, and the hours which preceded it, which she had shared with a terrified, brave little hunchback who had died on Midsummer Day, two hundred and twenty-eight years ago. For that was what it had said in the Bible, *deid the 24 Juin 1726 blottit owt of the Boke of Lyffe*. Anne felt her fingers straying towards the stone of power, and she felt weak with the wonder of it all. She also reflected, with trepidation, that there would be a lot of very embarrassing explaining to do.

But in this she was mistaken. When, rather sore, but otherwise recovered, she got up later in the day, Anne realized that her parents and Jenny had already decided what had caused her extraordinary behaviour the previous night. Soothing remarks were made about over-excitement, and the abnormal heat of the day, and the fearsomeness of the Bonfire. It was assumed that a combination of these elements had affected Anne's highly-strung body and vivid imagination. Which, in her view, was absolute nonsense, but she was relieved beyond measure that no one even tried to probe the nature of her experience. She was no keener now than she had ever been to suggest to these rational, unimaginative people that she was in possession of a talisman which could reveal the past, and cure many ills.

Before Anne went to bed that night, her mother said, 'No school for you tomorrow, I think. I want to keep you under my eye for another day. So sleep late, if you feel like it, then maybe you'd like to give me a hand in the skeleton's room? Very soon we're going to have to start moving all our finds to the Museum in Edinburgh, and I could do with some help in getting things in order.'

So Anne spent much of the next day quietly helping her mother to label pieces of flint, scraps of jadeite and slivers of potsherd, and lay them in order in the compartmented wooden trays brought from London for the purpose. And all the time she was aware of the infinitely old, infinitely unknowable skeleton lying on the board in the centre of the room. A woman who might have been important in her own day, Ben said, but who was now only an anonymous pattern of fragile bones, waiting to be numbered, boxed, and sent to a museum. All her secrets she would take with her; who she was, whom she had loved, how she had suffered, and how died, no one would ever know. Anne could not help comparing that blankness with the closeness she felt to Alice Jardyne, and for all the pain, she knew which she preferred. That was the day she decided that she did not want to be an archaeologist after all.

17

Another Point of View

The possibility that Polly might be cured of her paralysis through the power of the charm-stone had been in Anne's mind ever since the night when she had read, in Alice's own book, the names of those she had cured with it long ago. She had done nothing, partly because Polly did not seem to see the connection for herself, and partly because of her own fear that the power of the stone might have weakened during the two and a half centuries since it was last put to the test. Her own conviction that the stone was a magic one had never faltered since what she saw as the revelation of its ownership in Hoolets' Wood, but she had to admit that, until Midsummer Eve, its subsequent performance had been poor. It would have been too awful if she had persuaded Polly to try, and raised her hopes, only to have the experiment fail.

Now, however, all her doubts were swept away. After her experience in the Witch's Cottage, she felt that the power of the talisman had been proved beyond doubt, and she simply assumed that Polly, when she heard her story, would be convinced too. Everything had followed on so perfectly from the part of the story they already knew— surely Polly's disbelief would evaporate, and she would accept as historical fact Alice's flight from the drunken louts at the Bonfire, and her losing of the charm-stone as she struggled to hide herself in the Grey Mound of Deer.

So it was in great excitement that, on Wednesday afternoon, she walked the half-mile along the coast road from Marymount School to Maryfield House. The rain which had been sifting down like fine ash all day had now stopped, but it was very damp; conveniently enough, gardening would be out of the question. Polly was now so keen that it was difficult to get her to concentrate on anything else, when she could be out of doors in her straw hat and green apron, raking and watering and watching her flowers grow.

Today Anne found her in the drawing-room, sitting by the window in her wheelchair, reading a book about pest control.

'I think our phlox has got thrips,' she announced, then, looking at Anne anxiously, added, 'I hear you've been in the wars. Are you feeling better now?'

'Yes, I'm fine,' said Anne, taking off her hat and dropping into a chair opposite her. 'How did you know?'

'Sarah told me,' replied Polly, closing her book. 'She came for coffee this morning, on her way back from shopping. Laden with baked beans, as usual. She says you had sunstroke.'

'Yes.'

'Did you?'

'No, of course not,' said Anne impatiently.

'I see. Are you going to tell me what really happened?' asked Polly, after a pause.

Anne, who all through French, English, double Latin, Biology, P.E. and double Maths had been longing for the last bell of the day to ring, so that she could tell her, suddenly felt misgivings. Could she, after all, tell such a story convincingly? It had been such a very personal experience. Would Polly Jardine—grown-up, sophisticated and unimpressed by all previous evidence of the stone's power—really be converted now to belief?

'Poll,' she said slowly, 'if I tell you, will you try very hard to believe me?'

Polly looked at her with worried grey eyes.

'Oh, dear,' she said, shaking her nut-brown head. 'It's that kind of story, is it? I was afraid it might be.'

This was not encouraging, but Anne decided quickly that she had to go through with it. Without looking at Polly directly, she told her story, beginning with her having to dress as she believed Alice Jardyne had been dressed on

108

the last night of her life, and going on to detail her experience, between the time when she had sought refuge in the Witch's Cottage, and the moment when she had come round on the grass, beside the Grey Mound of Deer. She told it with passion and sincerity, for to her it seemed the most real thing that had ever happened, in all her life. 'So you see,' she concluded, half-pleading and half-assertive, 'the charm-stone *must* still be effective. I mean, you just couldn't have an experience like that unless you were under some sort of spell, could you?'

But when she raised her head and looked at Polly, it was obvious from the expression on her friend's face that she thought you could.

'If you are under a spell, Anne,' she said flatly, 'it's a spell in your own mind.'

'My own mind?' repeated Anne, uncomprehending. 'What's my own mind got to do with it, for heaven's sake?'

Pressing down on her hands, Polly eased her cramped limbs by changing her position slightly. She never felt really well, and now she was so weary she wished she had never heard of the charm-stone. But she was fond of Anne, and blamed herself for having fed, albeit unwittingly, her obsession with Alice Jardyne. So she tried to forget her aching back, and answered the question patiently.

'Everything, I should have thought,' she said. 'You see, whatever you may think, Anne, there isn't an atom of proof that any of your experiences were caused by a magic stone. You're not in the realm of King Arthur, you know.' This was hard, and Polly knew it was, but she thought it was something which had to be said. She paused, to give Anne time to remonstrate, but when Anne, slightly flushed, said nothing, went on, 'To go back to the beginning. One night, you had a dream about a wild girl being hunted through a wood. You yourself thought at the time that the dream was caused by your parents' finding a skeleton in the Grey Mound, and I still think that's the most likely explanation, if you must have an explanation at all. But then you changed your mind. Oh yes, I know you think the charm-stone disclosed the truth, but the only fact is that you changed your mind. After all, you were already far more interested in Alice Jardyne than you were in the skeleton, weren't you? And since then—admit it, my love—you've been interested in very little else. Apart from knowing what I told you—you've read Alice's book until you know it by heart, and you've done a whole study at school on the times she lived in. Can't you see that all these weeks you've been creating a mind-picture of Alice which—after a day of abnormal heat and stress—your own imagination brought to life?'

Again Polly stopped, and Anne could have begun to argue, but she was so upset that she felt the first words would choke her. So she sat pushing back her cuticles and trying to look nonchalant, and Polly continued. 'Up to this point, I sympathize with you. I've imagined her very vividly too, and sometimes she has seemed as real to me as people I know in real life. But what you're suggesting goes far beyond that. You seem to be saying that that pretty crystal bauble actually caused you to relive the last night of Alice Jardyne's life, and that you now know positively how the stone got into the Grey Mound. Am I right?'

'Yes,' muttered Anne, too miserable to sound defiant.

'Whereas I think we could only be sure of what happened if we found some documentary evidence. Your experience, which obviously was a very unusual and remarkable one, must be explained in a different way.'

'So you're not actually accusing me of lying?' Anne could not help saying bitterly.

'Certainly not. I never for a moment thought you were lying, Anne. Shall I go on?'

'If you like.'

'Well, then. I think the explanation lies in the power of your own mind. Not a power to be underestimated, either. You were tired and overwrought, disturbed by having to dress up and act a witch's part in the Pageant. You'd been thinking obsessively about Alice Jardyne, and you were actually sheltering in the walls of her house. The Bonfire reminded you of the flickering lights you'd seen in your dream, and as for the rest—if you honestly rethink your experience, Anne, I doubt you'll find a single element that you can't trace back to something you already knew. It's called suggestion. What happened to you has to do with psychology, not with a magic stone.'

There was yet another silence, during which Anne sat pouting and buffing the nails of one hand on the palm of the other. She wished she could think of some grown-up way of shrugging off Polly's opinion, as only one of several. But then she looked up, and saw Polly watching her with a white, stricken look on her face, and, surely, tears in her eyes.

'What is it, Poll?' she asked, alarmed. 'Don't you feel well?'

Polly bit her lip, and shook her head.

'I'm all right,' she said. 'It isn't that.'

'What, then?'

'It's just—oh, Anne, I'm sorry. I don't want to spoil anything for you. But it would be wrong of me to pretend to believe what I simply can't. And I do think it would be a good thing if you were to stop thinking so much about Alice Jardyne, and turn your mind to other things. Only— you won't be offended by what I've said, and stop coming to see me, will you?'

Then Anne, who loved Polly, got up and stood over her threateningly.

'Listen, idiot,' she said, 'I don't come here to do you a favour, you know. I happen to like you, although I can't think why, when you make cheeky remarks about the books I read, and you won't believe a word I say. Besides, I'd never get such good chocolate cake anywhere else, would I?'

These rude words reassured Polly greatly. She might have been reassured less if she had known that her careful, reasonable explanation had not impressed Anne in the least.

For, if Anne were under a spell, it showed no sign of releasing her yet. She did not even consider Polly's words seriously. With the memory of that terrible night when she had been Alice Jardyne still flooding her mind, the notion that it might have been caused by anything as tame as psychology seemed to her ridiculous. Her only regret was that Polly would not now have the pleasure of co-operating in her own healing; Anne was, however, determined to go ahead and cure her, whether Polly wanted to co-operate or not. Deaf to Polly's warnings, arrogantly disregarding her opinion and her wishes, she failed completely to see the dangers ahead. Convinced that the curing of Polly would be the climax of all these strange events, she fell asleep that night pleasantly imagining Polly's stunned delight, overwhelming gratitude, and apologies for ever having doubted Anne's word.

18

The White Glasse

Thursday was Polly's physiotherapy day, when she was too tired to see anyone in the afternoon, and on Friday Mrs Farrar took Jenny and Anne to the dentist in Dumfries. On Saturday morning, everyone had to help on the dig, so it was three o'clock before Anne was free to cycle over to Dunchree. During the three days since she had last seen Polly, her self-confidence had never faltered; she was the heir of Alice Jardyne, and miracles did happen. She took with her the charm-stone, a silver coin and a birch twig which she had cut from a tree in the garden of the Owls' House, and arrived at Maryfield House at half-past four.

It had been a warm, pleasant day, and Anne was surprised not to find Polly in the garden. Since the early days of their friendship, when she had been inclined to sit complaining that she was too disabled to do anything, Anne had encouraged her to rake and hoe, and to use the hose on her flower-beds. In the two little courtyards at the back of the house she had a flourishing pot-garden of herbs, fuchsias and geraniums, and Johnny had promised her a small conservatory next year, if he could afford it. Anne had told her father that accounts of John Jardine's wealth must have been exaggerated, since Polly said he was just a poor farmer. At this Dr Farrar chuckled merrily, and said that different people had different notions of where poverty began.

Failing to find Polly out of doors, Anne went into the house. There she did find her, lying on the sofa in the drawing-room. She had dark marks under her eyes, and Anne could see that, beneath the slight tan which she had acquired during her gardening activities, she was as white as a sheet. She was wearing her heavy metal callipers on her feeble legs and feet, and her crutches lay beside her on the floor. Anne knew how painful and exhausting Polly found walking, even from her bedroom across the hall to the room she was in now. She said she had to make herself do it, so that her muscles didn't deteriorate any further, but, Anne thought, she did not look as if she ought to have been doing it today.

'Anne, I'm sorry,' she said wearily as Anne came in. 'I'm afraid I don't feel well enough for gardening.'

'No, of course not,' replied Anne quickly. 'It doesn't matter a bit. What's the matter, Poll? You look terrible.'

This candour made Polly smile a little.

'Well, thanks,' she said. Then, 'I don't know, really. Just a doldrums day. I haven't been sleeping very well.'

'Would you rather I went away?' asked Anne, disappointed.

'No. That is, if you don't mind staying. I've said that Mrs Armitage may go to visit her sister in Dunchree for a couple of hours, since you're going to be here.' She paused, then said rather angrily, 'I'm not supposed to be left in the house by myself.'

Anne could understand how frustrating it was for a woman of Polly's age to feel that she was being treated like a small child, but she did not comment. Just sometimes, it was difficult to know what to say. And anyway—it wasn't for much longer.

'Shall I make us some tea?' she asked.

But there was an objection to this too, it seemed. 'Not for me, thank you. I mustn't drink anything while Mrs Armitage is out, or you may have to drag me to the lavatory.'

'That wouldn't upset me,' Anne told her, meaning to be reassuring.

'Perhaps not, but it would certainly upset me,' answered Polly, still with an angry undertone in her voice. 'Get some tea for yourself, though, Anne. I dare say you know where Mrs Armitage keeps the chocolate cake.'

With hindsight, Anne realized that the sensible thing

would have been to unbuckle Polly's callipers, tuck her up with a blanket, and encourage her to have a little sleep. Afterwards, it would seem incredible that with Polly ill and irritable, and with such a clear warning that she did not intend to drink anything in Mrs Armitage's absence, she should still have gone ahead with the healing charm. At the time, however, she could think of nothing else. Blind to Polly's real needs, she left her alone, and went off to hang up her blazer in the cloakroom beside the front door. She took the things she needed out of her pocket, and went with them into the modern, white-tiled kitchen.

Mrs Armitage had gone, so Anne had the place to herself. Taking the charm-stone from her neck, she laid it on the formica-topped table, and put beside it the delicate birch twig. Then she placed beside that the freshly-minted silver coin which she had been given the previous summer, as a memento of the young Queen Elizabeth's Coronation. The 'haire of an infant', also detailed in Alice's description of the charm, she had been unable to bring from home, but she knew where to find one.

A few weeks previously, Dr Farrar had delivered to the Jardines the wooden box, and its contents, which Anne had found in the hidden cupboard. Johnny had given the candlestick to Anne, and the box to Dr Farrar, who had admired it; the Bible and the lock of hair he had put on a shelf in his office, after Polly had grieved over them. *Haire of my sonne Johnne, dyed 2 yrs and 6 mths*—the child who had been Alice Jardyne's elder brother. Stepping lightly through the hall, Anne entered the office, took the tiny yellow package from the shelf, and carefully extracted one dry, flaxen hair. Holding it between finger and thumb, she went back into the kitchen.

And there, never for a moment pausing to consider that what she was doing was absurd or far-fetched, she drew the birch twig, the coin of 1953, and the hair of the little boy who had died in 1701 through a glass of tap-water. Then she solemnly dipped the charm-stone three times, reciting the spell aloud in the empty room. '*I shall dip thee in this water, thou clear gem of power, in the name of the*

115

Apostles twelve, in the name of the high Trinity, a blessing on the water, a healing to this hurt, and to this suffering creature.'

Then she had an idea. Carrying the glass carefully, she slipped out of the kitchen and into Polly's room. She went into the adjoining bathroom, opened the cupboard and found a bottle of aspirin, from which she took two tablets. Then she lifted the glass again, and went back to the drawing-room.

Polly was lying with her eyes closed, but she opened them when she heard Anne come in. If she had noticed how long Anne had been away she didn't mention it, but smiled at her, and said, 'Forgive me for sounding tetchy. Did you get your tea?' Then she noticed what Anne was carrying, raised her eyebrows and said, 'Oh, Anne! Surely we can provide you with something better than a glass of water. Why didn't you make a pot of tea, silly?'

Anne took a deep breath, and went and stood beside her. She held out the aspirins on the palm of her left hand, and the glass in her right.

'I shall, later,' she said. 'I'd rather look after you, first. I brought you these—I thought they might help you.'

Polly gave her an innocently grateful look.

'That was thoughtful,' she said, 'but I shan't, thank you all the same. I had some medicine at lunch-time, and I oughtn't to have any more until evening.'

Then Anne made the biggest mistake of judgement in her whole life. Oddly, it had never occurred to her that Polly might actually refuse to drink the charmed water. She had imagined Polly laughing, and calling her a baby, or shaking her head impatiently over what she saw as nonsense, but she had assumed that Polly would drink in the end. She knew how much her friendship meant to Polly, and never for a moment supposed that Polly would risk a quarrel. Blindly, she blundered on.

'Poll, listen,' she said. 'It isn't ordinary water. Please, drink just a little. I think it would do you good.'

'Do me good?' repeated Polly, bewildered. 'Why on earth should it do me good? Haven't I told you—' The

116

words tailed off, as comprehension slowly dawned on her pale face. An expression of amazement came and faded in her grey eyes, to be succeeded by a look of fury which made Anne quail. Too late, she remembered Polly's warnings about her own temper. 'What have you been up to?' The harshness of the voice made it almost unrecognizable. 'What's in that glass, Anne?'

'Just water,' mumbled Anne, cowering before the storm. 'Poll, I only wanted—' But Polly was not listening. Gritting her teeth, and pushing herself up painfully on her left elbow, she struck out hard at the glass with her right hand. It flew out of Anne's fingers, hurtled in a bright spray across the room, and smashed against a chest of drawers.

'How dare you?' said Polly, in a voice she was scarcely able to control. 'How dare you try to make a fool of me like this? Have I not been humiliated enough, without having a silly child making a game of me? Go away—no, please, don't say anything. Just go. I never want to see you again.'

There was no answer to this but to obey. Mustering what little dignity she could, Anne turned on her heel, and walked out of the room. She collected her blazer from the cloakroom and her silver piece and charm-stone from the kitchen, and left the house, resisting the temptation to slam the front door behind her. She cycled down the drive between the flower-beds she had planted, and made her way back to Deer with misery in her heart.

19

Reprieve

Sunday was an absolutely dreadful day. All the time that
her hands were busy, helping her father to pack the
interminable scraps of every possible material salvaged
from the Grey Mound, Anne's mind was in turmoil, as
loathing of her own stupidity and arrogance swept over
her in cold waves. It was not only that she was ashamed of
hurting Polly's feelings, and humiliated because she had
been called a silly child. Beyond self-deception now, she
felt that she had indeed been a silly child, until five o'clock
yesterday. At five minutes past five, she had grown up. For
then the sight of Polly lying impotently furious on the sofa,
wearing the tokens of her helplessness on her body, had
smashed for ever the world of make-believe where she had
lived for the past three months—where, she now realized
with raw self-knowledge, she had lived all her life. It was a
world which she would never inhabit again, in which
people had to be made more glamorous than they were,
where magic stones gave you glimpses into the past of
those who had been dead for centuries, and healed people
so terribly paralysed that any fool could see they would
never walk again.

For the first time, Anne forced herself to see Polly as she
really was, not an Arthurian princess, or a sweet nineteenth-century invalid like Clara in *Heidi*, but a brave yet
bitter woman, who had lost a baby and had her future
destroyed while she was still in her teens, and whose daily
life was an aching round of tiredness, loneliness and
frustration. That afternoon, Anne imagined what it was
like, being unable to wash and dress yourself without help,
having to wait for someone to bring you things because

you couldn't reach them, not even being able to go to the lavatory without someone to lift you on to it, and off again afterwards. And she acknowledged that she herself was not Heidi, the good little fairy who would make everything come right in the end.

To the end of her days, Anne would never really understand what had happened on that June night in 1954. Sometimes she would agree with Polly—although Polly would later modify her first opinion—that her own obsessed, overwrought mind had caused her experience. On thinking it over, she had to admit that every element could be traced back to something she already knew, or had experienced. Obviously, she had re-enacted the events of her own dream, and for the rest—the details of Alice's clothes, her prayer, the biblical words which had passed through her mind, the name, 'Marian Cunninghame', all had been in Alice's book, which she knew by heart. In the school library, she had seen pictures of cottage interiors at the beginning of the eighteenth century, and had read of the old Midsummer rituals in the book of Border folklore. She had learned that there was a space in the roof of the Grey Mound on the night when her parents had first shown her the charm-stone, and even the man in black, whom she had seen standing on the path, could, the grown-up Anne assumed, have had his origin in the figure of Apollyon, the foul fiend of *The Pilgrim's Progress*, whom Alice had drawn so starkly in her book. And yet— in a corner of her mind, she would always believe that there had been more to it than that, that in some inexplicable way, the spirit of Alice Jardyne had rubbed through time to find her. For the dream itself could never be explained, and the theory of coincidence could be strained too far. But one way or another, her encounter with Alice Jardyne, the obscure healer of Deer, was to determine the whole course of Anne's life.

Never again, however, did she consider that she had had a magic stone in her possession. With only the smallest pang of regret that she was severing a link with Alice, she gave it back to her mother, and watched the archaeologist putting it in a little cardboard box, dispassionately writing the date and place of its finding on the lid.

'It belonged to Alice Jardyne,' Anne told her, but Mrs Farrar was too busy to listen.

In the afternoon, when her father had released her from her task, Anne went upstairs, and wrote a letter of apology to Polly. She thanked her for her friendship and hospitality, and said she was sorry for the distress she had caused her. It was all she could do. She had no hope that Polly would ever want to see her again, or that Johnny and Mrs Armitage would allow her to, even if she did.

But in this, Anne was mistaken. In the evening, just after she had been to the postbox to post the letter, Steven Armitage roared up on his motor cycle, bearing a note and saying that Mrs Jardine wanted a reply. Anne tore open the familiar cream envelope with hasty fingers, and read, in Polly's jerky writing, *Dear Anne, I'm so sorry. I didn't mean it. I know you wanted to help me. Please come after school tomorrow. Tell Steven if you will. Love, Polly.*

'Tell her yes, Steven,' said Anne, hoping that he did not see the tears of relief welling in her eyes.

Steven nodded, and revved up his engine. He was a man of few words.

When she arrived at Maryfield the following afternoon, the first person Anne met was Steven's mother, normally a woman of many words. But today she was markedly cool. This did not surprise Anne, who knew that deserting her post had been just one of Saturday's sins.

'Mrs Jardine is in bed,' Mrs Armitage informed her shortly. 'She says you're to go in.'

Anne said nothing. She laid down her satchel in the hall, put her straw hat on top of it, and walked across to Polly's door. A scared glance told her that Polly was not having an afternoon rest; she was in bed properly. Anne went and sat beside her.

'I've made you ill,' she said guiltily.

'No, of course you haven't,' Polly assured her firmly. 'I was fool enough to cough on Saturday evening, and I've been here ever since. I have a chest infection. It's got nothing to do with you. Have you forgiven me?'

'I've no reason. I wrote to you—'

'I know. The letter came in the afternoon post.'

'Then you know how I feel. I was stupid and impertinent, and I'm very ashamed of myself.'

Polly smiled at her.

'Don't be,' she said. 'I should be grateful that you cared enough to want to help me, and indeed I am. Only—that isn't the kind of help I need, Anne. I need to be helped to accept being the way I am, not to be offered false hope of a recovery that can never be. Can you understand that?'

'Yes.'

'Then no more magic, my dear, please.'

'I gave the stone back to Mother,' Anne told her. 'She's put it with the other stuff she's packing up for the Museum.'

Polly looked relieved.

'I'm glad,' she said, 'for that's where it ought to be. It's only a museum-piece after all.' But then, as she looked at Anne, her expression changed, and her eyes filled with the sadness that Anne had wanted to take away for ever. 'Oh dear,' she sighed. 'Is Sarah really packing up at Deer already? I can't bear to think that you'll be going away so soon. I shall miss you so much, and I can't get used to the thought that I may never see you again. But it would have been horrible if we hadn't parted friends.'

Anne found herself staring at Polly in open-mouthed astonishment. Was it possible that she had never told her—well, obviously it was. But how strange.

'Poll,' she said, 'I thought you knew. I'm not going away. That is—I am, but only for a few weeks. I'll be back the third week in September. I've got to board at Marymount until I finish school.'

As she said it, and heard the words jerking out in a hard, gritty voice, she knew why she had never told Polly. Just mentioning it made her want to burst into tears. She saw the delight which had leapt into Polly's face fade, and concern take its place.

'Poor Anne,' she said. 'I'm sorry. Will it be so terrible?'

Then it all began to come out, how Anne hated the prospect of sleeping in a dormitory, and playing lacrosse on the sands, and Scottish country dancing, and walking out in a long grey 'crocodile' at weekends, and being supervised by prefects like Jenny every minute of the day. 'It will be like being in prison,' she said miserably, 'and knowing that you're just half a mile away will only make it worse. I'll only be allowed out two Saturday afternoons a term, Poll.'

She looked up, and saw Polly watching her from her pillows with sympathy in her eyes, but with a flicker of something else. Hope, maybe.

'But Anne,' she said, 'this is ridiculous. Why on earth should you board at Marymount, if you hate the idea so much, when you could stay here with us, and walk to school every day? Tell me—do Titus and Sarah want you to go to boarding-school particularly, or is it the teaching they approve of?'

'It's the teaching,' Anne told her, scarcely able to believe what she was hearing. 'I don't think they care about boarding, one way or another.'

'Well then,' said Polly. 'What about it? Shall we ask them?'

'Oh Poll,' breathed Anne. 'Do you mean it? Honestly? It would be the best thing that ever happened to me.'

Polly said that it would be a good thing for her, too.

'Three years,' she said. 'Johnny says it will take about that length of time to make the farms profitable, and pay off what we owe on this crazy house. After that, he's going to get a manager to help him run the farms, so that he can spend more time with me. But three years is a long time, and sometimes I feel very lonely, Anne. If you were coming in and out, it would be so different.'

'Then shall I ask Mother and Daddy tonight?' asked

Anne eagerly. She felt she could wait no longer for confirmation that this miracle would actually happen.

Polly considered for a moment, then she said, 'No. Not yet. Let me speak to Johnny first. I'll get him to come over to Deer tomorrow, and put it to them. Perhaps they'll think him a more responsible kind of guardian than me.'

Although, of course, she could not say so, Anne doubted this. She knew that her father and mother found John Jardine brusque in his manner, and thought that his only interest was money. If she were allowed to stay at Maryfield House, it would be because they liked and trusted Polly.

20

Alice Jardyne

When Anne came home from school next day, she discovered that her future had been arranged, just as she and Polly had planned. John Jardine had come in the morning; Dr and Mrs Farrar, shamed a little by Anne's intimation that he was working from dawn till dusk to pay off debts incurred in building a house for his wife, agreed readily that Anne should live with him and Polly for the rest of her time at Marymount.

Polly spent the next week, when she was still confined to bed, planning a room for Anne at the back of the house, overlooking the garden they had made. She made Anne choose what she wanted from books of wallpaper, curtain and carpet samples, and gave herself the pleasure of choosing the furniture. So, before it was time for the Owls' House to be evacuated, Anne had a perfect place of her own, hers for the rest of her schooldays, and a thousand times more to her taste than the poky cubicle in the Bluebell Dormitory which would otherwise have received her.

Meanwhile, the life of the Valley of Deer moved inexorably towards its ending. In the first week of July, tractors and trailers and chain-saws moved in, and the Valley sides were shorn of their forest covering, as high up as the level of the new Loch Dree. Hoolets' Wood was spared, as the timber was not worth cutting; it stood out, an irregular smudge of grey and green, against the hideous devastation of sawn-off roots and broken branches which the foresters left behind them. Anne could scarcely bear to look out of the window, and found herself almost longing for the day when the Valley would be sealed off, and the sadness of leaving would be over.

After her quarrel with Polly, and the relief of their making up, Anne thought less about Alice Jardyne than she had for many weeks. Perhaps this was because, with the future so much more attractive, she felt less need to seek refuge in the past; at any rate, it did no harm. Polly, who had been horrified by her insight into Anne's state of mind, shunned the topic completely; the weather was warm, and she and Anne spent most of their time together in the garden, where they were planting a rockery which Ben had laid out for them. But Anne did not forget Alice, and sometimes she wondered whether she would ever find out what the end of her story had been. She thought probably not, and this bothered her vaguely, as unsolved mysteries tend to do.

Then, one day, she did find out, in a strangely casual encounter with someone whose advice she had sought back at the beginning of her quest, over three months ago.

Term had ended at Marymount School on the twelfth of July. After that, Anne was at a loose end for a week, since Johnny had gone up north on business, and had taken Polly with him. On Wednesday morning she had gone to the churchyard to take farewell of the Jardynes of old, who would soon be resting at the bottom of a reservoir, and while she was there she met the Minister, Mr Russell. They sat down together on a toppled tombstone, and talked for a little about the paths they were to take, and which they knew would never cross again.

'Actually,' said Mr Russell, 'I've been meaning to come to see you, Anne, only I've been so busy I haven't had a moment. I wanted to tell you—that girl you were asking me about—Alice Jardyne. I can tell you what happened to her, after all.'

It was a perfect summer morning, with blue sky and a small breeze stirring the flower-splashed grass. High overhead, a skylark was singing, and nearer to hand Anne could hear the drone of bees in the froth of honeysuckle on the Manse wall. None of these changed. It was in herself, the feeling that the world had gone dark and silent, the deadening of the sky. Into this cold silence came Mr Russell's prosaic, Lowland voice.

'I was up in Edinburgh last week, for committee meetings, and I had some spare time on my hands. I remembered what you'd told me about the girl being blotted out of the Book of Life—an unforgettable phrase, that—so I thought I'd go along to the Record Office, and see what I could turn up.'

As simple as that.

He paused, obviously waiting for a word of eager encouragement from Anne, so she swallowed hard, and managed to say, 'And what—did you turn up?'

'Quite a lot, actually,' replied Mr Russell, pleased with himself. 'What wasn't in the Minutes of the Kirk Session was in the Records of the Courts that tried her. It's an interesting story, because apparently Alice Jardyne's was one of the earliest cases when a suspected witch was set free for lack of evidence—a 'not proven' verdict, we call it in Scotland.'

This was the last thing on earth Anne had expected to hear.

'Set free?' she repeated incredulously. 'When was she set free?'

'In March 1726,' said Mr Russell, fishing out a small black notebook from the inside pocket of his jacket. 'I took down some notes here—somewhere—yes. 1726, on the twenty-seventh of March—' The day her bedroom wall fell down, thought Anne, but did not have time to dwell on the coincidence. 'Apparently she had been accused by some superstitious old busybodies in this parish, and dragged before the Minister, who in those days would have been as afraid of witchcraft as they were themselves. She was arrested, and tortured in the Tolbooth at Kirkcudbright, before being taken to Edinburgh for trial before the Court of Session. But 1726 was late in the day for a trial of that kind. Belief in witchcraft was waning, at least among educated city-folk, and decent people were becoming sickened by the whole business of witch-hunting. A trial did take place, but at the end of it Alice Jardyne was set free, and sent back to her own parish.'

It was these words, 'to her own parish', which partially prepared Anne for what was to come. Alice would find no mercy in her own parish, whatever the judges in far-away Edinburgh might have had to say. Moistening her lips with the tip of her tongue, Anne said, 'What then?'

Mr Russell sighed.

'Ah, then,' he told her, 'I'm afraid the story gets very nasty. I've no idea what happened between March and June, but the Parish Records mention a disturbance which took place in the early hours of June the twenty-fourth. It seems that Alice Jardyne's reputation at home hadn't been affected by her acquittal in Edinburgh, and she was lynched by a mob from her own village. They tied her to a stake in the Water of Deer, downstream from the Bridge, where the river runs into the Loch, and stoned her to death.'

Anne was shaken by a revulsion so violent that she thought it must be visible. She wanted to scream, and stop him, but no sound came, and she had to listen as he went on, 'When she was dead, they untied her, and threw her body into that deep pool upstream that they call the Witch's Dam. A scandalous, wicked act, even for an uncivilized, backward place such as Deer must have been then. But it didn't go unpunished, Anne. The ringleaders were arrested, and tried, and hanged at Wigtown in December 1726. I noted their names, I think. Yes—Mungo Dick, a stableman, and Sanders Grahame, who was brother to Alice Jardyne's own sister-in-law.'

'That doesn't surprise me,' said Anne dully.

It was the other name that shocked her—Mungo Dick, who had received healing from Alice's hands, and had repaid her by leading the gang of thugs who had murdered her.

But Mr Russell was getting up to go. He must be thanked, and somehow she found words to thank him. If he noticed her white face and subdued voice, he did not comment, but said that he was glad he'd been able to help her.

'She was a brave woman,' he said in parting, 'though perhaps a foolish one. From the day when she was first brought before the Minister, until the day of her death, she refused to answer her accusers, or defend herself, even under torture. The Edinburgh judges thought she was a half-wit, although I doubt anyone around here would have agreed with them.'

Anne walked sadly home between hedgerows that had lost their colour, under an indifferent sky. That afternoon, she thought she could never be happy again. But her heaviest burden was the knowledge that she must tell Polly, when she came home at the end of the week.

21
Polly

On Thursday afternoon, Anne went up for the last time through Hoolets' Wood to the Witch's Cottage, soon to be submerged, yet visible, under the clear water at the edge of the new loch. Then it would become mysterious again, but now, in the sunlight of a July afternoon, it was unambiguous, merely a ruined hovel standing roofless in a heathery sea. Anne did not go inside, but sat for a while with her back to the sun-baked garden wall, listening to insects whirring in the leaves, and wondering whether Alice Jardyne really did spend the last day of her short life in this place, waiting in anguish for her murderers to come. She realized that she could never know for certain, but, since hearing Mr Russell's story, she found it difficult to imagine any ending to Alice's story, other than her having been taken by her drunken, hate-crazed pursuers as she struggled to hide herself in the Grey Mound of Deer. Whether it had happened that way, or whether she had unwittingly arranged her knowledge to make a story, as an ending it was horribly plausible.

Then, as the remembered horror of being Alice began to blot out the sun, Anne got up in a hurry, took a trowel from the basket she had brought, and began delicately to pry up roots of primrose and cowslip to be transplanted into Polly's garden at Maryfield. When she had wrapped the plants in newspaper soaked in the spring that bubbled through the heather near the cottage door, she went down the hill without looking back. She was glad that she had rescued the plants for Polly, who would like to have them; but she never wanted to see that place again.

On Friday evening, Steven arrived with a note for Anne. In it Polly said that she had had a lovely holiday, and asked Anne to come on Saturday afternoon, and to stay overnight. Anne replied that she would come early on Saturday evening; the family was now packing up at the Owls' House, and she knew that she would have to help, before escaping to Dunchree. Their work almost done, the Farrars were now looking outward from the Valley, Jenny to the pre-nursing course she was going to take, Dr and Mrs Farrar to a new excavation they had been asked to undertake in Wales. Even Anne, who loved the Owls' House most, noticed with a sense of shame at her own fickleness, how the centre of her life had already moved to the house and garden at Maryfield.

So she spent Saturday patiently helping to pack books into boxes for London, and blankets into boxes for Wales, obeying orders and using the quiet beyond the chaos to work out how she might most gently break to Polly the news of the death of Alice Jardyne. For it was not something she could hold back; however painful the intimation, Polly would also prefer to know.

At six o'clock, she put her night-things into the saddle-bag of Jenny's bicycle, and hung the basket of plants over the handlebars. Then she made her way up the shorn, disfigured Valley's side, and down the winding hill road to the house by the Bay.

It was a mellow, golden evening, and Polly, looking lovely in a new pink dress, was in the garden, cutting withered heads from geraniums which had bloomed in her absence. When she saw Anne, she put down her shears and moved her chair into one of the courtyards, inviting Anne to bring a deck-chair.

'I'm glad you've come,' she told her. 'Johnny has gone up to the farm at Glenwhirn, and he'll probably stay the night. So I thought we could have fish-pie and a good talk.' Then she caught sight of the basket which Anne had put down on the grass, and added, 'Anne! You've brought me something new, haven't you? Tell me what it is!'

130

'I got some primroses and cowslips from the cottage on Cairnshee,' Anne told her.

She did her best to smile at Polly normally, but seven years of observing the reactions of others had sharpened Polly's own responses, so that she knew something was wrong. She gave Anne one of her penetrating looks, and said quickly, 'What's the matter, Anne? Has something happened?'

'Not exactly,' Anne replied.

She had spent most of the past three days trying out forms of words in her mind, searching for one which might be used to communicate to Polly, without hurting her terribly, the end of the story of Alice Jardyne. Only now she realized that none of them would do. There was no way of imparting such news without giving distress. She must simply tell Polly what she knew, and try to comfort her afterwards. So, with only the warning, 'This is horrible, Poll,' she repeated the story which Mr Russell had told her. And when it was finished she knelt beside Polly, and they put their arms around each other, and shed tears, and grieved for the death of a friend.

'What I can't understand,' said Anne, when they had dried their eyes, and she had returned to her deck-chair, 'is why she didn't try to defend herself. She was innocent, Poll. Why didn't she tell them—at least try to make them understand? Mr Russell says she didn't put up any fight at all.'

'Oh, I think I can understand that,' said Polly soberly. 'I expect by that time she simply didn't want to go on living in a world she had ceased to comprehend. All her life she had put good before evil, and other people before herself, yet in the end she saw evil triumphant, and the very people she'd tried to help leading her enemies against her. I'm sure she felt she had absolutely nothing to live for. I've been close to that kind of despair myself, but it's different for me. I have Johnny, who still loves me, in spite of everything, and my parents, and my sister. She didn't have anyone. Rob, whom she loved most, was too cowardly to lift a finger to help her, and Janet and Isaac were afraid to

131

involve themselves—they said because they had children. It's the same argument people used in Germany twenty years ago, to excuse themselves from helping their Jewish neighbours. Whether or not you think it's an adequate excuse depends on your point of view.'

Anne looked gravely at Polly's thoughtful, intelligent face.

'What do you think, Poll?' she ventured.

Polly spread her thin hands in an uncertain gesture.

'I hope I'd have been brave enough to stand up for my neighbours,' she said, 'but of course you never do know how much courage you have, until you're tried. When I think of Alice Jardyne, I realize how very lucky I am.'

At fourteen, it had not yet occurred to Anne that the future might repeat the mistakes of the past. Meaning to be comforting, 'I suppose we must just be thankful that such things can't happen nowadays,' she said.

Polly shook her head.

'We must never allow ourselves to think that,' she said. 'Think of the concentration camps in the war, Anne. Only nine years ago, my father was with the troops who liberated Belsen, and the horrors they found there wouldn't lead you to suppose that human nature has improved at all since the seventeenth century. In 1700 it was witches, in 1945 it was Jews. As soon as another minority is seen as threatening the majority, however falsely or unfairly, it will happen again.'

These sad, uncompromising words disquieted Anne, but she had no answer to them. It was the first time she had faced the possibility that the second half of the twentieth century, which would be her lifetime, might not after all be a Golden Age, when all wrongs would be put right.

In the cool hour before night, Anne and Polly planted the flowers from Alice's garden in a sheltered corner, and watered them. Then Anne wheeled Polly indoors, and they ate their supper by the window overlooking the Bay. They were both tired, and didn't talk much, but they were glad of each other's company. At ten o'clock Mrs Armitage came to help Polly to bed, and Anne went off to her own room. She slept better than she expected, and woke to another clear day.

After she had eaten her breakfast in the kitchen—Mrs Armitage having declined to carry trays, now that she was to be a member of the household—Anne went to Polly's room to say goodbye, just as she had on that first Sunday morning in May. She found Polly as she had then, sitting up in bed with the Sunday newspapers spread out around her. But there the similarity ended, for when Polly raised her head and smiled at Anne, Anne had the strangest sensation that she was looking at someone she had never seen before. All the habitual strain and sadness had gone from Polly's eyes, there was no flickering frown between her brows, and her nervous, fretful hands were perfectly still. Anne went and sat beside her on the bed.

'What is it?' she asked uncertainly. 'You look different, Poll.'

'Yes, I'm sure I do,' said Polly, wonderingly. 'I feel different. I'll try to explain, if I can.' She was silent for a moment, as she often was when she was trying to put her thoughts in order, but then she said, 'Anne, I think I owe you an apology.'

'Do you?' said Anne. 'Whatever for?'

'You remember, when you had that strange experience on Midsummer Eve, I told you that it was all the product of your own mind.'

'Yes.'

'Well, perhaps I was wrong. Or perhaps the power of the mind is more amazing than I ever imagined. You see, last night I had a strange experience too.' Anne was too astonished to say a word, and Polly went on, 'It was like this. After Mrs Armitage had got me into bed, I asked her to put out the light. Usually I read for a while, but my head ached, and I knew I wouldn't be able to concentrate. I didn't suppose I'd be able to sleep either, but I just wanted to be quiet, and alone.

'For a long time, I lay thinking over what you had told

me about Alice Jardyne's death, and imagining the fear and pain and desolation she must have suffered. And I was ashamed, because I knew it was the first time in seven years that I'd ever grieved properly for anyone, other than myself. I'd often thought that Alice would understand how unhappy I felt, but I'd never seriously tried to put myself in her place. I think I cried for a while, but then I must have slept, because when I awoke it was dark—darker than it ought to be at this time of year. I felt—what's the best word? Expectant, perhaps, and as if all my senses were strained, yet I couldn't even see the shapes of the furniture, or hear a whisper of sound. And then—oh, it's hard to explain, because I didn't see her, or hear her, but I felt that Alice was in the room with me. And it seemed that she was telling me not to be afraid, because all was well with her, and all would be well with me, too. I don't know how long it lasted, but I must have fallen asleep again, because the next thing I knew it was morning, and the sun was shining across the bed. The sense of her presence was gone, but the reassurance she'd given me was still there. Of course, I know that many things in my life can never change, but I think from now on I'll find them easier to bear.'

Anne looked at her with happy eyes.

'I'm so glad for you,' she said sincerely.

Polly rested herself for a while, then she said, 'I've never been able to come to terms with what happened to me, Anne. It all seemed so unfair—unfair to Johnny, and to our poor baby, as well as to me. I've tried not to make a fuss, and to put on a brave face for the sake of the people who have to cope with me, although I haven't always achieved even that. I've felt so angry and bitter, and jealous of everyone who can lead a normal life. There have been times when I've hardly been able to look at my own sister's children without hating her. But this morning, I feel renewed. Oh, I can't wait for Johnny to come home!'

22

Rites of Passage

On the last day of July, huge notices appeared beside the roads entering the Valley, warning people that after the tenth of August entry would be prohibited, and the area sealed off. During the next week, sheep and cattle were rounded up and driven to safe pasture elsewhere, convoys of carts and vans left for the new village up behind the dam, and birds hovered above a waiting and desolate land.

On the third of August, a van arrived from the Museum in Edinburgh, to remove the crates of artefacts and hundreds of photographs of the Grey Mound of Deer. The Farrars would finish writing their account of the excavation when they got back to London, and before they went to Wales. Anne sat on the sun-warm wall at the kitchen gate, watching as the four-thousand-year-old skeleton, discreetly boxed, left for its last, unthinkable resting place in the heart of a modern city. A queen, perhaps, among her own people, the woman remained nameless to the last, a subject only for learned speculation, blotted out of the Book of Life. Whereas Alice Jardyne, the obscure farmer's daughter whose name had lived, despite all the odds, would not suffer the fate which her malevolent sister-in-law had wished upon her. For she would be with Polly and Anne always, in the garden, and in the world beyond where Anne would spend her life.

The last Sunday came, and the church bell of Deer rang out sweetly, calling the congregation to the final service in the little church. Dr and Mrs Farrar had decided that they ought to attend on this occasion, so, with Jenny and Anne, they joined the solemn drift of parishioners converging on the churchyard. They received a guarded welcome from the elders in the porch, and Mrs Farrar, who for a year had been criticized for not coming to church, was now criticized for coming without a hat. The family slipped into a pew near the back, rather wishing they hadn't come, until, at the very last minute, and to Anne's intense delight, Johnny and Polly arrived to join them. Some of Polly's newly-found happiness seemed to have rubbed off on to her husband; it was hard to recognize in this relaxed, smiling young man the stiff, shy person they had hitherto encountered.

Anne scrambled eagerly over everyone's knees, so that she could sit at the end of the pew, with Polly's wheelchair beside her.

'You look smashing, Poll,' she said enthusiastically, admiring Polly's soft blue jacket and tiny hat covered with blue and white flowers. Then, 'I never thought you'd come.'

'Neither did I,' admitted Polly. 'But at the last moment, we decided that this was where we wanted to be.'

The organ wheezed, and began to play. Mr Russell climbed into the pulpit in his plain black cassock, and the service began. 'Let us worship God. Let us sing . . .'

It went on for a long time, with Bible readings and repeated, inevitable references to Noah's flood. Children became restless, old people drowsed in the stained-glass sunshine, Dr Farrar and Johnny teased a spider which had come out of the woodwork, and was scuttling about on the book-board, trying to get back in.

But Anne was glad to be there, with Polly beside her. She felt that she had come to the end of a long journey, and was a different person now from the one who had set out. With a new tolerance, she perceived that these dour country-folk—even if they had lived all their lives in a bowl, as their ancestors had done, and thought it was the world—had an inkling at least of something which the clever Farrars failed to grasp, that there might be a mystery beyond themselves.

Afterwards, they waited in the churchyard while the huge Bible, and the Communion cups which had been old when Alice Jardyne was born, were carried from the Church to the Manse. There they would be kept safe until tomorrow, when they would be taken to the Church at Kirkton, which the Valley exiles would now have to attend. Then Jenny sprinted home in a panic, because of course her mother had invited the Jardines and Miss Groom to lunch, and of course they had accepted, and of course there were only the dregs of the Three Varieties, and four eggs in the pantry.

The Farrars were to leave Deer on Monday morning, to go first to Dunchree to say goodbye to Polly and Johnny, and then to Kendal, where they would spend the night with friends. Dr Farrar reckoned that, provided they were not held up for hours in long ribbons of holiday traffic, edging nose-to-tail through Preston, Manchester and Leicester, they might make it home to London by midnight on Tuesday. But before they left the Owls' House, Anne had one more thing to do, and on Sunday evening, when Jenny was over in the cottage, helping Ben to finish his packing, she went to the study and put her head round the door.

The night had turned chilly, and Dr Farrar had lit a final fire on the hearth. He and his wife were sitting in front of it on the sofa, holding hands, but they made room for Anne, who went and sat between them.

'There's something I want to tell you,' she said.

'Oh, dear. You're not in love, are you?' asked her mother, only half-laughing.

'No,' Anne told her. 'It isn't anything like that. It's—well, if I told you I didn't want to be an archaeologist after all, would you be very upset?' Their unperturbed faces answered this question, so she went on with more confidence. 'You see, I've been thinking. It isn't that I'm not interested in the past, because I am, and I always will be. Only I don't think now I want to live in it. I want to do something which has a long tradition, yet will help to make a better world in the future. I'd like to study medicine, I think.'

Impossible, and unnecessary, to tell them that she wanted to follow in the footsteps of Alice Jardyne, whose desire to heal had been thwarted by the ignorance and superstition of the age she had lived in. Anne would achieve through scientific knowledge cures of which Alice could not even have dreamed.

Dr Farrar voiced a thought which was in his wife's mind, too.

'You can't cure Polly, Anne.'

It went through Anne's mind that he didn't know the half of it.

'I know that,' she said. 'I can't even help to prevent there being more Pollys, because there's a vaccine now, and in a few years there won't be any new cases of polio, thank goodness. But there are other illnesses where they haven't even begun to find cures. I think I'd like to have a part in finding them.'

'Then you'd like to do research?' asked her mother.

'If I'm good enough,' Anne said.

Mrs Farrar nodded, then she said thoughtfully, 'You know—when I was a young woman in the early twenties, and my father was a clergyman in Sheffield, I saw the poverty and squalor and disease which were the lot of the poor in those days. Children with rickets and tuberculosis, men and women old and worn out before their time. Sometimes I felt guilty that I hadn't chosen a profession where I could have helped at least some of them. But the truth is that I wouldn't have been any good at it.' She laughed, and added, 'So perhaps that cheeky little Minister is right—my social conscience is self-indulgent, and all I can do is talk. However—nothing would give me greater pride than to know that both my daughters were working to make sure that those terrible times could never come again.'

'Daddy?' said Anne.

Dr Farrar put his arm around her.

'Anne,' he said. 'Believe me—if I know that you're happy, and doing what you want to do, and using your intelligence to the full, I don't mind what career you choose.'

Anne got up then, and said that she would go and see whether Ben had managed to get his suitcases shut yet. But at the door she turned round, and saw that her mother and father had already closed up the space where she had been sitting.

'It isn't fair,' she complained. 'Everybody is in a pair, except me. There's you two, and Johnny and Polly, and Ben and Jenny. I'm the only single left.'

Her parents seemed to find this very amusing.

But, 'I wouldn't worry too much,' her mother said, when she had stopped laughing. 'You've got plenty of time. I didn't marry Tich until I was thirty-four.'

The Farrars had overheard Jenny and Ben talking one evening outside the kitchen window, and had been calling each other 'Tich' and 'Sadie' ever since.

'And then she only married me because I had a better prismatic compass than she had, didn't you, Sadie?' said Dr Farrar, giving his wife a squeeze.

It was Jenny who said they were like children, but sometimes Anne agreed with her. Rolling her eyes, she closed the door, and went out of the house into the yard. Thirty-four, she thought, as she crossed the cobbles under a thin white moon. She wasn't going to wait until she was thirty-four. That was middle age.

And then, pleasantly, she remembered that in the autumn Johnny Jardine's seventeen-year-old brother, Richard, was coming on a visit. Polly said it was high time for Anne to meet a nice young man.